M000305789

WILL TRIPP GOES
HOLLYWOOD

A terrifying journey deep into
the land of WOKE-THINK!!!

WILL TRIPP GOES
HOLLYWOOD

A terrifying journey deep into
the land of WOKE-THINK!!!

FEATURING GENDER STEREOTYPES! DOG WHISTLES! PATRIOTISM!
(with a special guest appearance by HATE SPEECH)

Proudly presented by **HARRY OLIN** ~~CANCELED~~

Copyright ©2021 Harry Stein. All rights reserved.

No part of this book may be used or reproduced in
any manner whatsoever without prior written consent of the author,
except as provided by the United States of America copyright law.

ISBN: 978-1-7351928-0-2

Published by

The Calamo Press
Washington D.C.

calamopress.com
Currente-Calamo LLC
2425 17th St NW, Washington D.C. 20009

For Andrew Breitbart

"Your honor, may I approach?"

Judge Lucas raised a bushy eyebrow. "What is it now, Mr. Tripp?"

Will Tripp signaled to the bailiff, who produced the stepladder Will habitually used in court, and set it before the bench. Especially with women jurors, it served as a sympathy-inducing prop, emphasizing the dwarf lawyer's pluck in seeking to overcome his disability.

He smiled gamely at the jury as he struggled to mount the two steep steps, the prosecutor looming huge and menacing alongside. In response, the jury foreman nodded encouragingly.

Will had taken care to stack the panel with men middle-aged and older; and of the two women, one was the mother of twin boys serving as the president and vice president of the leading fraternity at the Midwestern university once named by *Playboy* the nation's top party school, and the other was a tattooed, bristly haired long-distance trucker who had, Will's investigator ascertained, recently joined a dating site called Find Femmes.

On the other hand, Judge Lucas was a problem from the start. Though a middle-aged white man himself, the judge was also, more importantly, a committed "progressive," or at least believed it was vital to his career prospects that he be seen as one; and he viewed this case, with its vast media interest, as an unprecedented opportunity to show off his feminist *bona fides*.

Little wonder the judge had been keeping Will on the shortest of leashes. He knew that the dwarf attorney brought to his work not just verbal dexterity, but relentlessness and guile; and that representing as he did only one species of client — victims of political correctness run amuck — he was capable of pulling almost any tactic in their defense.

Since the start of the trial, Judge Lucas had been repeatedly crimping Will's style with sharp reprimands, while sustaining the prosecution's every objection.

Indeed, in the midst of his questioning of his key witness — the defendant herself — he had just been slapped down again.

"Your honor," he said now, atop his ladder and eye to eye with the jurist, "with all due respect, I need to be allowed to delve into this poor woman's background for the jury to appreciate that her behavior was not only appropriate but..."

"Mr. Tripp, she seduced *nine* of her students!"

"...not only appropriate, but laudable!"

"Mr. Tripp, I will not..."

"And it was seven. The other two heard about it and propositioned *her!*"

"Mr. Tripp, you're trying my patience..."

"Your honor, I must be allowed to introduce evidence of the indignities Ms. Applebaum has endured, the abuse, the pain, the victimization…"

"What indignities, what pain?" heatedly countered Scott Schmidt, the prosecutor. "She's the perpetrator here, not the victim!"

"*What pain?*" shot back Will, incredulous. "The pain faced by every soul with her disability!"

"What disability?"

"The disability of a face and body that might have been painted by Rubens!"

They stared at him momentarily, trying to decipher this.

"A-plus body, B-plus to A-minus face," elaborated Will. "I'm talking the pain of being *objectified!*"

"This is your defense?" said the judge.

"A key element, your honor – that as men *we* are the guilty ones, not her. I intend to call scholars…" — Will almost choked on the word, knowing how hideous were the shrews from prestigious universities he'd lined up — "whose research confirms it." He indicated the defendant with a sweep of his tiny hand. "I urge caution, gentlemen: Do you suggest Ms. Applebaum, alone among women, has escaped the ravages of patriarchy?"

Despite themselves, the judge and prosecutor cast a glance at the defendant. Will had dressed her in nondescript gray pants and a heavy black sweater, her blonde hair was in a bun, and her posture in the witness chair suggested back trouble.

"Go on, look," said Will disgustedly. "I saw you both staring at her ass when she walked in...." He paused meaningfully. "...And so did the jury."

"Is that a threat, Mr. Tripp?!"

"Do I look like that kind of man?" responded Will noncommittally.

He began his descent, then stopped on the middle step, turning back, as if something had occurred to him.

"What?" demanded Lucas.

"My client requests that the temperature be lowered."

"Excuse me?"

"In the courtroom."

"I didn't hear her say anything."

"Will you not at least give her that? Testifying is extremely stressful under the best of circumstances; being made to do so in this heat constitutes cruel and unusual...."

"This conference is over, counselor," the judge cut him off. "I'm quite sure Ms. Applebaum can endure another half hour of 72-degree temperatures. Now can we get on with it?"

"Of course, your honor."

"Good, resume your questioning of the witness."

Reluctantly, Will climbed down from his perch.

"Now, Ms. Applebaum," said Will, striking the pose so familiar to devotees of his courtroom theatrics – feet planted firmly apart, thumbs in suspenders à la Darrow, three foot six of deadly self assurance, "let's go on to Charlie Everts, the young man in your Algebra II class."

"Yes," she said softly, dropping her eyes in a show of modesty.

"Speak up, Ms. Applebaum, I know this isn't easy for you." He paused. "Now, this young man, Charlie, can you describe to the jury the initial impression he made on you?"

She looked at him quizzically. "The impression he made? I regarded him as a student, like any other."

"Not as a stud?"

"Objection!"

"Withdrawn. And as time went by? Did your opinion of this strapping young fellow begin to change?"

Schmidt started to rise, but Tripp quickly added: "Did it change?"

"I saw he was a fine student."

Imperceptibly he ran his tongue over his lips; imperceptible, that is, to all but the witness. Signal received.

"Is that all he was to you, a fine student?"

"No," she allowed, in her evident nervousness fumbling with the top button on her sweater, "also a fine young man."

"You *respected* him, then."

"Very much so," she said, undoing the second.

"An *attentive* student?"

"Absolutely."

"Interested in the work – and, by extension, in you, as his instructor…"

"It was my job to encourage him," she allowed, undoing the next.

"Your job to *encourage him*," repeated Will for emphasis, turning to the jury. "Encourage the young man. That's the goal of every good teacher, isn't it?"

"Yes, I've always thought so."

"Of every *great* teacher. Of Plato. Of Socrates. Of the learned men – and, yes, the women! – at our own great universities! To encourage the student to the maximum of her abilities! Using every means at her disposal!"

But his words were now secondary, in fact, scarcely heard, for he knew that behind him the witness had removed her sweater, and that the blouse beneath was of sheerest silk.

Suddenly, in a gesture he knew would insure the jury's attention was where it belonged, he wheeled and pointed an accusing finger at the witness. "Ms. Applebaum, what have you done? What have you been about here?"

"I took off my sweater."

"Who gave you permission to do such a thing? Have you no sense that it impinges upon the dignity of this court?"

"I'm sorry," she said with contrition, "I was hot."

Will paused thoughtfully, allowing this last to linger a moment, then turned back to the jury. "I'm sorry, I was hot," he repeated. "*I'm sorry, I was hot.*" He paused again; the old guys were riveted, a couple even on him; the long distance trucker was nodding. "Gentlemen and ladies, that, right there, is the essence of this case. As a result of circumstances entirely beyond her control, Ms. Applebaum is…"

"Mr. Tripp," the judge cut him off, "I'm not a fool, I can see what you're doing. This line of questioning, if that's what you call it, is over. The nature of the defendant's...presentation, her...physicality..." He paused, quickly adding "...or lack thereof, is not at issue. We are dealing in facts!"

"Your honor, with all due respect, I submit that Ms. Applebaum's hotness is not only a *fact*, but a fact entirely beyond her control. I further submit that as a strong and independent woman, through no fault of her own endowed with qualities esteemed by the oppressor class, to attack her on this basis is out-and-out discrimination!"

"You accuse this court of being anti-woman?" shot back Judge Lucas, stealing a worried glance at the assembled reporters.

"I do no such thing," Will retreated slightly. "Surely you will concede, your honor, as will Mr. Schmidt, that there is an ingrained bias against women in this country!"

Schmidt leapt to his feet. "I move to strike! If anyone present in this courtroom is biased against strong women, it is counsel for the defense, who has consistently mocked and belittled..."

"That's enough from both of you," shouted Lucas, banging his gavel.

"Afraid of women?" thundered Will, ignoring this. "What are you talking about? I AM a woman."

There was a momentary stunned pause.

"What did you say, Mr. Tripp?"

"That is my chosen identity. For the remainder of this session."

"That is patently absurd."

"Is it?" countered Will, his voice rising to a shrill, feminine pitch. "Why would you deny me the right to be whatever I choose to be?"

He stole a quick glance at the jury, and was pleased to note several were smirking. He saw that the judge saw it, too.

"That's ENOUGH, Mr. Tripp."

"Ms. Tripp…"

"No, *Mr.*, unless and until you are able to prove otherwise to my satisfaction." He banged his gavel. "Court is adjourned. Now you will have Ms. Applebaum put on her clothing."

"Certainly, your honor. Only it's *Mr.* Applebaum. And please call me *they*."

Back in his office, on the 45th floor of the Chrysler Building, Will swung his hand-tooled boys size 8 ⅝ cowboy boots onto his desk, leaned back in his custom-built Techni Mobil ergonomic executive chair and fired up a Cohiba Behike.

Life was good – in a way. Business was booming. Never had he been so busy.

Then, again, there was also the reason why: his enemies were everywhere rampaging through the culture, befouling everything that was good and decent in life.

Famously, Will's mission in life was to stop them. No attorney in America was more careful in his choice of clients. He represented only those who had run seriously afoul of mindless PC and its noxious enforcers: bureaucrats issuing freedom-crushing diktats; social justice zealots at what formerly were institutions of higher learning; union thugs; pussified corporate executives.

Like hollow-eyed refugees of a century past fleeing the murderous totalitarianism of Europe, into this office streamed those desperate for his services; more of them now than ever, each with a new horror story. Sitting at his desk, listening, Will mourned the vanished America into which he'd been born, one that admired character and scorned victimhood as the province of those doomed to failure and ignominy.

He glanced now at the framed movie poster on the wall opposite: *The Man Who Shot Liberty Valance*. Jimmy Stewart and John Wayne. One, the intrepid book-totin' lawyer risking death at the hands of a psychopath to bring decency and order to the lawless West; the other, the cowboy who casts aside personal happiness for larger principle.

Odd, Will mused now, that all his favorite movies had "man" in the title. *A Man for All Seasons…Cinderella Man… The Man Who Would Be King*.

Well, okay, not *Caddyshack*. Or *Groundhog Day*.

Maybe it was either "man" or Bill Murray.

But he also had to acknowledge, at least to himself, his mounting frustration; there was just too much idiocy out there and – let's call it what it is – *evil*. The bad guys simply ran too much of the world; for all his passion, he could scarcely put a dent in it.

There came a soft knock on his office door, almost more like a caress, and instantly recognizable.

"I'm decent!" he called, swinging his legs off the table to sit upright in his chair.

"That's not the word on Twitter…" said Cheryl Knox, smiling, as she set his daily whiskey sour — Crown Royal and egg whites — on the desk before him. "They're very unhappy with your behavior today."

"Ah," he said, raising the glass. "Success!"

He withdrew another cigar from his inside jacket pocket. "Join me?"

Taking it, she sat in the chair opposite.

"Two more calls from horny school teachers – California and Colorado," she said. "They sent pictures. If you're interested." She lit up. "I don't even know why I bother adding the last part."

He snapped his fingers and she handed him her cell phone.

Cheryl was more than just a personal assistant; she was an auxiliary conscience. Lately she'd been trying to convince him he probably should not take any more of these cases; too often they were seen as demeaning his other work. Cheryl even had a theory about why many of these women were so good looking – having been love objects in high school, they were continually trying to replicate the experience.

He respected her perspective and, in truth, really did not need much convincing. He'd begun taking on these cases as a means of attacking that which he found as repellant as anything in the noxious PC universe, the progressive war on biology – male biology in particular – but by now he was repeating himself.

Then, again, he also knew the point couldn't be made strongly enough.

"I should at least meet Ms. Ortiz," he said, studying the photo and the accompanying write-up. *Anita Ortiz, Mexican-American, five foot ten.* The photo showed her in tight jeans, hand on hip, back to camera, peering saucily over her shoulder. "She seems to have the stronger case."

In short, Will was a complex man and, yes, a romantic. For as long as he could recall, he was liable to find the very sight of an attractive woman profoundly moving, and he was feeling that way now. Famed as he was for his poker face in the courtroom, one thing he did not have was a poker pecker, and he was grateful to have the desk above him impeding her view.

Fortunately, his phone sounded — the theme to *Perry Mason*; the original show, where the crime was always a nice, neat murder, and justice always triumphed in the end, not the psychotic piece of crap remake on HBO. God, Hollywood, there was truly the root of all evil! The dwarf lawyer snatched it up. Noting it was from Brunswick, Maine, where he knew no one, he answered in the whiny, addled old woman's voice he liked to summon up for phone solicitors.

"Helllooo," he screeched amiably at the recording. "I should press one? ... Oh, dear... Okay."

Though the voice struck Cheryl as less old womanly than androgynous, it was certainly annoying, and deeply disturbing. She watched, amused, as she dimly heard a man with a Pakistani accent pick up on the other end of the line. "Hello, my name is Bob, may I please have the year and model of your vehicle?"

"Yes, Bob, I DO want an extended warranty," enthused Will, "I was *hoping* you'd call again!"

The crook on the other end of the line seemed startled. "Thank you, sir…Can you tell me the year and mod…"

"Did you say 'sir?'"

"…madam…"

"Welllll… it's a 1999 Honda Civic. It has, let me see, 397,000 miles…"

There was a pause. "I'm sorry, do you possibly have a newer…"

"But I need the extended warranty right away, the transmission's not so great."

By now, the solicitor was trying to get off.

"I don't understand," wailed the dwarf, in distress, "you call me every day, and every day I say, yes, and then you tell me no!" He listened a moment to the other's protestation. "It doesn't help me that you're sorry. Just please, *please*, give me my extended warranty!"

The Pakistani hung up and so, smiling at Cheryl, did Will. "You'd almost think they don't want my business."

"You really are bored, aren't you?"

"I prefer 'restless.'" He took a sip of his drink. "So, anything else?"

"You're not going to like this. Or maybe, under the circumstances, you are."

He gazed at her inquiringly.

"Remember, you've got that interview with *The New York Times*?"

"Oh, Christ!"

"…In half an hour…"

While his feelings varied according to circumstances and his ever-shifting moods, all in all journalists consistently ranked high on Will's list of the world's worst people; higher even than the vile denizens of the academy, now everywhere busily injecting their poison into the culture at large. For the media maggots were the universal enablers; who, having been charged with guarding the immeasurable treasures of free speech and free thought, had instead, in their hideous weakness, or overweening ambition or, worse, genuine solidarity, thrown in their lot with the vandals. The only ones worse, arguably, were the witless celebrities with the titanic presumption to inflict their toddler's understanding of the world on the rest of us.

"Who this time?" he asked.

Not that it mattered. All of them played the same game of "gotcha," or at least tried.

"Name's Adam Marsh."

Will nodded, dimly recalling the byline. One of the new breed of candy-assed kids who'd been raised on the PC crap.

"Get me his bio and a few choice clips."

Twenty-eight hundred miles away, Sue Sawyer was in the sunlit study of her Hollywood Hills home, aimlessly scrolling through her laptop, when she heard the front door open, and tensed.

"Michael?" she called.

Her husband didn't answer, but when he entered the room, she knew: the meeting had been a disaster. Mike Sawyer's was an unusually expressive face, he'd made a good living with it for a long time, but what it registered now was not mere disappointment or even resignation. It was hopelessness.

"There's nothing," he said tonelessly.

"Nothing *at all?*"

"'*No one* wants you.' His exact words. He didn't even have the decency to sugar coat it. Or maybe the decency not to."

"Jesus, Mike!"

He gave a mirthless laugh. "Probably not even Him."

Not, of course, that it was a total surprise. It doesn't take tea leaves or mind readers to sense the industry turning against you; just someone's sudden aloofness, or no longer getting calls and texts answered. Hell, Noah Field had dodged him three days before agreeing to this meeting; and even then he'd had Mike come by the office, rather than taking him to lunch at Toca Madera or Soho West or anyplace else they might run into someone.

And Noah was not just his longtime agent, but his closest friend in town.

"Noah!" said Sue, shaking her head bitterly. She'd always been inclined to red hot passion, his instinct was conciliation.

"Not his fault. Don't blame him."

"I do. He could fight it, he could stand up and..."

"Stop!" he cut her off. "And do what? He's also got to make a living." Then, more gently, he added: "Remember... Truman."

Both were admirers of the 33rd president, and his famous remark – "If you want a friend in Washington, get a dog" – was part of their private shorthand, reserved for times like this.

Except there'd never been a time as bad as this.

"Washington's nothing!!" she said. "Here the dog would leave you the instant someone offered him a tenth point more of the gross. And bite you on the way out!"

He managed a smile. "After shitting on the carpet."

"And telling himself how good and moral he was."

The fact is, everything had happened so quickly, it was still hard to get their heads around it. Only a week ago, Mike had been doing just fine. Better than ever, in fact. He'd just wrapped the second season of the Netflix series, *Cry Babeee, Cry!* as the cranky but loveable father of the sex-mad female teen protagonist, and was about to be re-upped by Providential, the insurance conglomerate for whose commercials he'd fronted for the past several years. Indeed, with his mix of good humor and quiet strength, Michael had that trustworthy thing going in spades, and he was a familiar, comforting presence to millions who'd never seen him anywhere else. In his negotiation with the company, Noah had deftly used surveys showing Sawyer was as closely associated with the Providential brand as the Gecko was with Geiko.

Most meaningful of all, he'd just been signed for what he hoped would be his breakout part on the big screen: the role of Andrew Jackson in *New Orleans*, billed by the studio as an "updated retelling" of America's astonishing, against-all-odds victory in the battle of that name at the close of the War of 1812.

It was the break he'd been waiting for since they arrived in Hollywood nearly 20 years ago. While the script took a few dramatic liberties, turning the bellicose and pitiless Jackson into a man anguished about the foundational sin of slavery and sickened to the core by bloodshed, it was the rare chance to play a deeply complex figure; potentially Oscar material! Moreover, in showing how the future president threw together a coalition of frontiersman and free blacks, Choctaw Indians and spirited buccaneers to beat back the highly trained British invaders, it was something even rarer: a movie that seemed almost pro-American.

Indeed, on first reading, Michael had wondered how that obstacle had been overcome and the picture green lighted.

Surely the diversity angle would not have been enough. But then he learned — and this only added to his excitement — that the town's most bankable star, Marc Guerin, a Louisiana native, had signed on as the swashbuckling pirate leader Jean Lafitte.

But now *New Orleans* was gone, too, along with the rest. And the irony was that the instrument of his destruction was the same Marc Guerin.

He may not have been the one who initiated the assault — that was the anonymous bastard who out of the blue posted a photo of the American flag flying in front of the Sawyer's house — but it was Guerin's message later that day to his millions of followers that was the hammer blow.

It had come after a second anonymous poster cited a remark the actor reportedly made in reaction on the set of *Cry Babee, Cry!*: "What's wrong with flying the American flag?"

"I am shocked to learn of the words and actions of Michael Sawyer, with whom I now learn I was to appear in a forthcoming motion picture. I want those who have earned my trust to know that will not happen. I will never lend my name or reputation to any project in which any such individual is involved. Trust me on this! Yours in solidarity, Marc."

By day's end, the hashtag *@FireFascistPigMichaelSawyer* was closing in on a million hits.

Now, as her husband reported on the gruesome particulars of the meeting with his agent, Sue's mind drifted. What the hell to do now? Vanessa was midway into her freshman year back East at Chester College; and while they'd had a number of concerns about the place, starting with whether it might turn her into some version of the kid in his Netflix show, until now footing the more than 100 grand per annum had not been one of them. They'd bought this house just six months before, at the top of the market, and had put in a deposit on an extended rental for a condo in Steamboat Springs; though neither skied, Noah said it was a great place to get away from it all, and also a great career move, because so many Hollywood players also vacationed there.

Hers had always been the lesser career, her last regular paycheck having come four years before, when she played the nosy neighbor for a season on a Fox sitcom, but who could doubt that, caught in the undertow, her days as a potential earner were also over.

When he'd finished, she quietly asked, "Did you defend yourself?"

"To Noah?" he shook his head miserably. "Really, Sue, what would be the point? You know how these things work."

"As your agent, he should *do* something! They're making you out to be a monster, and you're not."

"Actually, to them, a lot of them, I am."

And it was true. Though he'd tried to be careful, he was among the few in Hollywood who'd maintained a discreet silence when others were denouncing wrong-thinkers in the media, or marching in the streets, and otherwise flashing their moral *bona fides*.

"You think Noah likes this?" he asked. "He doesn't." He reached into his jacket pocket, and pulled out a folded sheet. "He thought maybe this could help."

He put on his glasses and read. "I am deeply aware of the pain I have caused, and I am profoundly remorseful. As disappointed as they are in me, I am even more disappointed in myself. Both my grandfathers fought in World War II..." He looked up. "I made him put that in."

"Good."

"... but that is no excuse. Nor is the fact that it is an old photograph.

The damage my actions have done to my friends and colleagues is inexcusable, and I have no one to blame but myself. I have always told my daughter to stand up and admit her mistakes and now I am doing the same. I know by my actions I have defended racism, sexism and homophobia. I am ashamed over how uninformed I was."

She stared at him a long moment. "I don't think so." She paused. "These pathetic apologies never work."

"Right. It was just an idea." He gave a helpless shrug. "Tough day, I'm beat..."

"Go upstairs. Take a Xanax."

"Right. Love you."

She listened to him trudge up the steps.

Closing her eyes, and took a deep breath — *Those motherfuckers!* — then reached for the pad with the scrawled name: Will Tripp (212) 722-5400.

The reporter showed up several minutes early, as Will knew he would. Kiss asses from the word go, these idiots were as predictable as maggots in a garbage dump. Not *too* early – that might look unprofessional – but definitely never, ever a second late. From little kids so eager to answer teachers' questions their arms look about to pop from their sockets, to the Ivy Leagues, then straight into elite newsrooms, every move they'd ever made was a calculation, and God forbid they'd risk an independent thought.

"Mr. Tripp," said this one, when Cheryl ushered him in, thrusting out his hand, "Adam Marsh, *New York Times*."

Will stayed in his chair, making the reporter come to him before offering a limp hand.

"Thanks for seeing me, Will."

"Oh?"

The other looked momentarily confused.

"Have we met before? Are we friends?"

Behind his MOSCOT glasses, the reporter's eyes flashed unease. "I don't think so."

"Even close friends dare don't call me by my first name. Not to my face."

"I'm sorry," he stammered, though he knew this had to be a lie.

Not having been invited to sit, the reporter stood awkwardly for a long moment, as his host sized him up.

Around thirty. Longish hair, already thinning. Sneakers, black chinos, dark sweater over button-down shirt. In the old days at least they wore jackets and ties, but not these creeps.

"Cigar?" offered Will.

"No thank you, I don't smoke."

Will nodded approvingly. "Right, vile habit."

Will lit up, inhaled and blew out a gust, making the other visibly shudder.

"I won't take much of your time, I just have a few questions."

"Take all the time you need," said Will magnanimously, "I have the highest regard for the media."

"Thank you."

"Mind if I ask you a couple first?"

"Uh…No, I guess not."

"Where'd you go to school?"

"Me?" He perked up. "Yale. Then Columbia School of Journalism."

"Good. Impressive. You did well?"

"I did okay," he said, confidence returning, "I was always a pretty good student." He flashed his faux modest shit-eating grin. "So about *my* questions…"

Will held up a small hand. "Just a couple more." He paused. "What can you tell me about the Erie Canal…"

"The *Erie Canal?*" he said, perplexed.

"When was it built, what was its purpose?"

There was more to this than just mischief making. A history buff himself, it was Will's conviction that every citizen should have a passing grasp of the country's past and founding principles; and especially those in the media, bearing as they do special responsibility for the preservation of the republic. Yet it was his *experience* that, more than those in any other field, reporters took self-regard to be a fit substitute for such knowledge.

But mainly, it was mischief making.

Will smiled sympathetically as the journalist wrestled with the query.

"I mean, of course I've heard of it." He paused. "I really don't get what that has to do wi…?"

"You're right," Will let him off the hook, "that was a pretty hard one." He thought a moment. "You heard of the Civil War?"

"Yes," he said with exaggerated patience, "I have heard of the Civil War."

"Excellent! Tell me when it began and ended. Month and year."

"Mr. Tripp, I really don't think…"

"Or World War I. Your pick." Watching the journalist's brow furrow in concentration, Will added, unnecessarily, "Bet you know about 1619."

"Oh, sure, *absolutely*," he said, brightening, "that was when the first enslaved people…"

"Then you naturally also know the year Lincoln freed the *slaves*," the dwarf lawyer cut in, stressing the now-forbidden term.

His visitor took a deep breath, summoned up his professional voice. "Mr. Tripp, I am not here as an historian, but as a journalist…"

"I'm sorry. Of course." He stubbed out his cigar and leaned earnestly forward. "I'm a firm believer in the First Amendment, it's the rock of our freedom."

"Thank you. I agree."

"Do you? Good." Will motioned. "Please, have a seat."

"Thank you," he said, starting toward the chair.

"Not there." Will pointed. "There."

"On the floor?"

"If you would." Then, earnestly. "It's a Little Person thing."

"Oh. Sure."

Gingerly lowering himself to a sitting position, the reporter crossed his legs, yoga style. "No problem."

"Hold on, now I can't see you. Move that way."

There was a soft knock on the door and, opening it, Cheryl saw the reporter scuttling crab-like across the floor. She generally disapproved of Will's humiliation game, but just now she couldn't help appreciate the genius of its execution.

"Don't interrupt, Cheryl," he said sharply, though her appearance was by pre-arrangement. "Mr. Marsh was about to tell me what he knows about the First Amendment."

"I'm sorry, sir, but we'll have to cut this short. Call you should take." Moving closer, she slipped before him the message from the distraught woman in California. But what she whispered, with urgency and deep concern, loud enough for the reporter to hear, was what they'd decided on earlier. "The lab just came back with the Applebaum results!"

"*What* results?" demanded Marty Katz, looking up from page four of *The New York Times*.

"Had to give the little bastard something, couldn't send him back to his editor empty handed." Will took a sip of coffee and smiled. "Keep reading."

Katz looked back down at the paper. "Nonetheless, before the trial went to the jury, resulting in yesterday's acquittal, Tripp submitted no lab results of any kind to the court. 'Whatever they were, they went right out the window,' noted one longtime close observer of the theatrical attorney's methods, speculating that the findings might have established that the boys shared drugs with their teacher, Ms. Applebaum, prior to the alleged sexual encounters. 'For Tripp, justice is always secondary, winning is everything,' he added. 'He's a stone-cold liar, and I've seen him do worse.'"

Katz looked up again, the light of sudden understanding behind his tortoise shell glasses; Will's closest friend, he was someone who *really* knew the man and his methods. "It was a set-up!" he said in near-awe.

Will confirmed this with a modest nod. "Already talked to Leslie Applebaum, poor woman's distraught! Can you imagine? Defamed in the country's most important paper *after* being proven innocent!"

The table erupted in laughter.

The five others gathered in Yonker's Euclid Diner were Will's unofficial brain trust, and they'd been getting together weekly since back when the dwarf lawyer's office was around the corner on South Broadway.

Alongside Katz, Will's perpetually harassed and often despondent landlord pal, sat his Mexican-born private investigator, Danny Valenzuela. Then, too, there were Will's longtime legal associates, wheelchair-bound Marjorie Spivak and the hulking Arthur XXX Perkins. Though neither was more than marginally competent in the practice of law, both were invaluable for other reasons. Even when the facts of a case looked bad, Spivak, bravely struggling from her chair and lurching toward the jury, instantly sent the sympathy factor soaring – and that was before they heard her stutter! And Will was yet to meet a liberal juror who, watching the imposing dashiki-clad Arthur XXX at the defense table, scowling menacingly, did not covet his good opinion; nevermind that in real life Arthur was a country club Republican who favored cashmere sweaters and pastel polyester slacks both on and off the links.

Will's brother Bennett rounded out the group. A physics professor at upstate Chester College, he'd arisen at dawn to make the 8:30 breakfast. Never a picture of confidence even as a younger man, Bennett had been permanently de-balled by his years in academia, and Will was sometimes startled by his utter stupidity. Still, for that reason, he could be especially useful at these sessions, parroting as he did, on a range of subjects, the "thinking" of America's intellectual class with which Will had to contend.

Sure enough, alone among those at the table, Bennett now flashed sudden concern.

"Problem, Bennett?" prompted his brother.

Avoiding Will's gaze, Bennett pushed around his scrambled eggs on his plate. "No...I guess not."

"Jesus Christ, out with it! *What?!*"

"It's just, you know..." ventured Bennett, "It's...*The New York Times.*"

"Fuck 'em!" said Katz, the landlord, knowing from hard experience that the paper's editors yearned for nothing so much as to get him and his into tumbrels, bound for oblivion. "Lie through their teeth and think they're untouchable!"

"*The New York Times v. Sullivan,*" nodded Will. "You people know the case?" He turned to his associates. "Arthur? Marjorie?" Both stared at him blankly. "It's their big escape hatch – foundational libel law."

"A fucking blank check, is what it is," muttered Katz darkly.

"Says they can print any damn thing they want about someone as long as it's a 'public figure,'" confirmed Will, making quote marks with his tiny fingers. "Think Leslie Applebaum suddenly qualifies as a 'public figure' just because some horny kids lied about her?"

"Sounds like libel to me!" agreed Katz with relish.

"Libel *and* reckless disregard," came back Will, "with a fat dollop of 'actual malice' on top!"

The legal lingo further fueled Katz's ardor. "Do it!" he urged, wild-eyed.

"I'm thinking about it, I'm seriously thinking about it. Think your friends in real estate might be interested in funding a case like that?"

"Bet on it!"

"Oh, God," whimpered Bennett, anticipating, as always, the reaction on campus.

"This gets us into what we need to talk about," continued Will, "— where we go next." He paused to take some pages from his briefcase, and briefly flipped through them. "Possible new cases." He glanced at the top page — "Sexy teacher " — then the next – "Sexy teacher. I got nine of these."

"I like those cases," volunteered Valenzuela. *"Me gustan mucho esos casos,"* he repeated, for emphasis.

"I know that," acknowledged Will, who strongly suspected his trusty P.I. may have fulfilled a couple of his own boyhood fantasies in the course of investigating them. "Then, again, how 'bout this…?' He pulled out a page, scanned it momentarily, and held it aloft. "A ten-year-old boy whose parents decided when he was four that he wanted to be a girl and…"

"Don't say it," shuddered Arthur XXX.

"Gone, lopped right off." He paused. "So do I represent this kid against his parents – who, by the way, cashed in by writing a book featuring their own sensitive and caring selves

— *Jack to Jill, a Mother's Story*?" He looked around the table. "Tempting, no?"

He pulled out another page. "Whistleblower fired by Twitter."

And another.

"Whistleblower fired by Google."

And another.

"Whistleblower fired by ESPN."

Will paused dramatically before displaying another page. "Then there's this. Breach of contract case in California." He paused meaningfully. "Bingo!"

Around the table, the reaction was as expected: befuddlement.

"A breach of contract?" said Valenzuela dubiously. That was a job for a paper pusher, not the swashbuckling shrimp beside him; not to mention, what the hell would be a *P.I.'s* role in such a case?

"It's all very preliminary. I need to meet with the guy first, and his wife — she's the one who called. And the guy wants a look at us."

"*He* wants to interview *you*?" said Katz. "Screw that! Who the hell does he think he is?"

"He thinks he's Michael Sawyer."

There was a momentary pause — the name rang a bell, but a very faint one.

"It ain't luck, it's Providential," intoned Will, imitating Sawyer's calmly reassuring tag line in the commercials.

"*That* guy?" said Katz.

"Great company, Providential," enthused Arthur. "I had a fender bender one time, they got me a check in two weeks."

"Yeah, well they got an opening for a spokesman, maybe you should apply. 'Cause they dumped Sawyer."

"Wait," pressed Valenzuela, "you're saying we're off sexy teachers cause some actor lost his commercial gig?"

"It's *why* he lost it." He turned to his brother. "Bennett, they teach about the Hollywood blacklist in that crappy school of yours?"

"We have four courses on it! Horrible! People losing their livelihoods, for nothing more than expressing their beliefs."

"Wait, hold on," Katz interrupted sharply, "this guy's not a commie, is he?"

"So what if he is!" countered Bennett fervently.

"Actually, the opposite," Will told the landlord. "Apparently that's his problem."

Will opened his briefcase and withdrew a contract page, several signatures visible at the bottom. "This is a movie he was supposed to be in. Until last week."

"What is it?"

"A big deal. Co-starring Marc Guerin."

"Mmmmmmmmarc Guerin?!" shrieked Marjorie.

Will looked at her, startled. He had expected dropping the star's name would bring a reaction, but not this one, and not from this quarter. "You like him?"

"Oh my Ggggoddddd, he's soooo hhhhhot!"

"Yeah, well, bastard's number one on our enemies list. So you could get to meet him."

She looked at him closely, eyes aglow, scarcely daring to believe. "I'm ccccccoming?"

Will nodded. "Might have to gut him like a fish and need your help."

"Yes!" she exclaimed, thrusting a clenched fist upward in triumph.

"You, too, Arthur."

Arthur nodded soberly — "Yessir" — but his fleeting smile betrayed he was already making plans to play Angeles National, Riviera and Penmar.

In fact, the dwarf attorney didn't yet know how he'd use them, just that he was embarking on a venture unlike any he'd undertaken before, into the very cradle of suffocating right-think, to take on those blithely undermining the values and traditions of the country he loved, and the whopping virtue signaling firepower of his A-team helped his chances.

"How thrilling for you all," said Valenzuela acidly, "getting to rub shoulders with all the big *estrellas de cine*!"

"Counting on it, Danny," came back Will. He patted the P.I.'s arm. "Relax, don't I always find something exciting for you to do?"

The first thing that struck Will as his Cadillac Escalade limo pulled up before the Sawyers' home was that the place was nothing more than a simple one story bungalow.

"This it?"

"Yessir, seems to be – 4907."

"Christ, almighty," he exclaimed, having had Cheryl check it out on Zillow, "*this* is all 4.8 million buys out here?"

The driver, a would-be actor, snorted his agreement. "Unbelievable, right?"

Taking his attaché case, the lawyer slid off the seat and seized the door handle. "Sit tight."

Moving up the walkway, he noted a FOR SALE sign beneath the bright pink azaleas, and rang the bell. He recognized the voice responding within as Sue Sawyer's. "C'mon in, it's open."

Nice, the easy informality boded well for their working relationship.

When she appeared from around the corner, she was wearing the same tailored jacket she'd had on for both their preliminary calls, but in person she was better looking; the kind that comes with a healthy diet and lots of time in the gym. In her late 40's, she was trim, and probably still turned a few heads.

But looking more closely, Will saw the stress she'd been under beneath her vivid blue eyes.

"Thank you for coming," she greeted him, extending a hand.

"Glad to be here."

"You're alone?" she asked in some surprise.

He nodded. "My associates are out seeing the sights — first time out here for both. You'll meet them soon."

In fact, he'd instructed Marjorie and Arthur to stick close to the hotel, itself far in the Valley; he might need to spring one or the other on someone as a surprise.

"So…" Motioning, she led him to the living room, done up in Midcentury Modern.

"Nice place."

"Thanks, I did a lot of it myself." When he didn't reply, she added, "Didn't even bring in a decorator 'til a few years ago, and that was only to help with the accents."

"Ah."

"When we first got out here, we really had to watch our nickels and dimes."

"You've been here how long now?"

He was just being polite, he already knew; as well as that they'd come from Kansas City, after meeting in college; and that her own career had also shown promise, but never amounted to much.

"Oh, goodness, almost 20 years now, seems hard to believe."

"I notice you've put the house up for sale."

"Yes." She sighed, possibly for effect. "We're not sure there's much alternative…"

He wasn't about to give her any reassurance, not yet, at least not until he had scoped things out. But he'd already let her know he was doing this *gratis*. This was his policy; it was what rich, freedom-loving friends like Marty Katz were for.

"Can I get you something to drink?"

"A beer would be great," said Will, thinking it might be early – both in the day and their association – to ask for a whiskey sour.

"Oh, I'm afraid we don't have any alcohol here. But we do have some excellent exotic fruit juices. Limonata, Xango, Pampelmo?"

Great, he thought, nodding pleasantly, so she's a lush – or, worse, her husband, the client. Maybe both. Which could definitely be a problem for the case. "Water would be fine."

"Aqua Pinna?" she asked, turning toward the kitchen, "Essentia? Electrolyte?"

"Your call."

By the time she returned he'd hoisted himself onto a low, swervy couch, designed without concern for even a normal person's comfort, and Will was perched precariously on the narrow edge of a curve, feet dangling, having to hold tight with both hands.

"Careful, that's an original Piccarelli," she said, setting his glass on the Nike swoosh shaped table alongside. "My designer found it at a wonderful little shop on Melrose."

She took a seat opposite, and exhaled. "Well...Again, thank you."

"Michael's not going to join us?"

"He's in the bedroom," she said, nodding vaguely in that direction. "He's a bit...you know...."

"Of course, it's been a rough time."

"...depressed. Very deeply, actually. He's seeing someone about it."

"I see." The effort to look sympathetic was a stretch for the dwarf attorney, his own life credo being *Shut up, and get on with it.* "I'm so very sorry."

"She has him on Valdoxan. It seems to be helping, at least some."

Will nodded, making a mental note: great, a drunk *and* a lunatic.

"His first instinct was to fight back, that's who he is."

"Of course."

"But now...I don't know, it's like he's given up."

Fearing she might tear up, Will averted his eyes and reached for his glass.

Amazing — the stuff was terrific, a remarkable mix of flavors, one of them definitely mango, his favorite!

"So I'm just going to have to do the fighting for him," she added with renewed command. "They said for better or worse, and I guess now's the..."

"I understand. But since Michael's the client, I want him involved with…"

"He will be. He just needs some time."

"Okay." Releasing his grip, he cautiously dropped onto *terra firma*, and assumed a casual pose, elbow cocked against the seat of the Piccarelli. "I, of course, understand my job is to be there for *both* of you, make you *both* whole."

"Thank you," she said with emotion, then paused a moment. "Do you think we can win?"

He nodded. "I'm hopeful. I wouldn't be here otherwise."

But he was far from ready to elaborate, both because he genuinely did not know and because they might well have a difference of opinion about what winning meant. Her interest was in saving her husband's career; his, as always, was in making the larger point about freedom of thought and speech and, if possible, hitting back hard at the bastards who abused their power to deny those things to others.

It was a vital distinction, and one he would have to deal with eventually. But not now.

"It's completely obvious, isn't it, that they violated Michael's *New Orleans* contract," she said, a statement, not a question.

He nodded. "That will certainly be helpful."

She looked at him questioningly. "Just *helpful?*"

He saw no need to sugar coat it. "Unfortunately, any contract can be broken. Or at least an effective argument can be made for breaking it. It's the reason corporations keep some of the most shameless whores of my shameless profession on staff."

"I know that, but the language in this one..."

"And, from what I understand, the studio legal departments use the most shameless of the shameless..."

"God, sometimes I really hate this town!"

"I don't doubt it," he said, pleased; it was vital they be on the same page.

"We're not even very political people."

"Really?" Now, *this* was useful information.

"But these people sit in holy judgment! They can lie and cheat all day long, and go to sleep believing they are the best, most moral people on earth!"

Better and better; the chip on her shoulder was almost as large as his own.

"Well," he offered reassuringly, "exposing hypocrites is what I do – hypocrites, bullies and all-purpose assholes."

"Thank you," she said again, "Michael and I just hope..."

She stopped. Right on cue, her husband was in the entryway. He was dressed in red striped pajamas and what Will recognized – he had a pair of his own, boy-sized — as Ugg slippers.

"Michael, this is Mr. Tripp, the lawyer we discussed."

"How are you," he said, flat-voiced.

"Not bad," said Will, thinking *a helluva lot better than you.*

Sue went to his side and gripped his hand. "Thank you for joining us."

Sawyer did not reply.

"I think this could be an important case, Michael."

The guy nodded.

"We feel a lot better having you on our side," Sue spoke for them both.

That sounded like an exit line, and he'd seen enough. "I'm glad," he said, walking toward them. He shook her hand, then his; it was soft and lifeless. "You should," he added.

As she led him out the door, he turned back to her, making like it was an afterthought. "You know a good photographer?"

"What for?"

He didn't answer, musing instead: "Actually, we should probably also get some video."

Will was never cruel, unless intentionally, and he didn't have the heart to say what he was thinking: the media loved nothing more than before/after stuff. "Before" was set – until the Twitter assault, this zombie was among TV's most beloved and good humored pitchmen, but he'd need an "after" set to go if the guy offed himself.

Danny Valenzuela was strolling down Lower Broadway, a meatball wedge in hand, when his phone sounded. Setting the sandwich down on a window ledge, he rubbed tomato sauce from his fingers onto his jeans, and snatched the phone from his shirt pocket,

As usual, Will spoke without preamble. "Look into Marc Guerin. Hard."

"*Jesucristo, hombre*," came back the P.I. in not quite mock annoyance, "ever think I might have other stuff going on?"

Will guessed — accurately, it turned out — that the investigator had been using the time to explore the allegations against the latest batch of accused teachers. "I know that, Danny. But I really want to nail this bastard."

Valenzuela responded in kind. "What are we after? He's just an actor, what do you expect to find?"

"Start with the basics," said Will briskly, "the stuff on public record – his background, key relationships, both business and personal." He paused. "Arrests, or course, and perversions…"

The P.I.'s fingers were working the keyboard. "You look up Guerin on the web, you get over four billion hits…"

"So there's gotta be some great stuff."

The P.I. laughed mirthlessly.

"Don't worry, 99.9% of it's just bullshit — fan pages, or stuff about his movies, or the incredible rags to riches story of Marc Guerin as dictated by P.R. hacks to hack journalists. His journey from the Louisiana swamps to…."

…But there's still that tenth of a percent." He paused. "Do I have to stroke you? Need to be reminded you're the best there is?"

"That, and how about giving me some idea of what the hell this is about? I've never even seen one of the guy's movies."

"Course not, you're not a Millennial or a Gen-XYZer or whatever stupid name they've come up with for the next bunch of morons. You also don't believe in the religion of global warming or say 'enslaved peoples' for slaves."

"Meaning?"

"Bastard's got a personal mob of Twitter followers. Sawyer's only the latest victim. Someone needs to make an example of this guy."

"Right." He paused; intensity wasn't his style or, normally, his friend's either. "So, think you might use Marjorie on this?"

"There's an idea," said the dwarf attorney with a laugh.

"Get her close enough to the guy, she'd probably rip his clothes off on the spot."

"Except on his worst day Marc Guerin does better than Marjorie by accident."

Still, it was a vivid image – and, if it came to that, one that would horrify any jury. Even as he shut off his phone, Will was filing it away in the back of his mind.

Eager as she was to be helpful, Sue Sawyer hadn't guessed her attorney's purpose, so she had gotten the details wrong. Will had expected to find her husband dressed in the pajamas and slippers in which he had last seen him. Instead, as she led Michael haltingly into the living room, he saw Sue had dressed him in the Rural Everyman garb he habitually wore in the commercials, checkered red flannel shirt and comfy jeans.

"Ready for our close-up, Mr. DeMille," she said, with awkward good humor.

"Great," replied Will. "How you holding up, Mike?"

"Fine."

"He's feeling better," confirmed his wife, "aren't you, darling?"

"I am," he agreed.

In fact, it suddenly struck the attorney that the garb – presenting a version of the man at once familiar and disconcerting — was, however inadvertently, an inspired choice.

"Well, you're an old pro, this should be a snap." Will indicated the one chair in the room that suggested any possibility of comfort, and motioned for Michael to take it. "We'll just have a conversation, no big deal."

The camera was already in place, on a tripod before the chair. Will had instructed Evan, the kid operating it, the son of close friends of the Sawyers who ordinarily did weddings and bar mitzvahs, that Michael was to be mainly shot from the waist up, but he should be on alert to move in close on his ravaged face for enhanced emotional impact.

"Got it," noted Evan, with a brisk nod, "medium shot to tight shot, do it all the time."

Evan had also brought along a Nikon P1000 to shoot stills. Will wanted these in black and white, with shadows emphasizing the hollows beneath the actor's eyes.

Michael took his seat.

"Okay, honey, all set?" said Sue brightly from the side, and Will was surprised to see him shoot her a fleeting look of annoyance. He was aware of being treated with condescension, and even in his diminished state, didn't like it.

Will immediately factored this into his own approach.

"So, Michael," he began, from his place alongside the camera, "let's start with a little background? Can you tell us how you got involved in this crazy business to start with…?"

"Well…" he said uncertainly, "…it's a little complicated."

"I understand you grew up in the Kansas City area."

"Yes. Mission Hills, Missouri."

"And you went to the University of Kansas."

"I did." There was a long pause, and Will was about to instruct Evan to shut off the camera so they could start again. "I started doing theater there," he said suddenly, "I loved it."

"You decided you wanted to make it your profession…"

"I thought…" – he smiled, again unexpectedly – "…I could do a little good with my life. Maybe make the world a little less grim."

Here, however fleetingly, was the wry, self-depreciatory Michael Sawyer the world knew, and was impossible not to like.

At the attorney's prompting, he talked of the plays he'd done in college, and how he'd met Sue there, and how, after a couple of years working on and off in New York theater, they'd decided to come out West.

It could have been the story of any of a thousand actors in L.A., differing only in the particulars, but the particulars were not without interest, and Michael seemed to grow increasingly relaxed in the telling. More important, they got the attorney where he wanted to go: to the sledgehammer that had lately come down on the Sawyers out of the blue, just at the moment when he was poised to achieve the great success he'd worked for all these years.

The attorney signaled for Evan to move in tighter, then paused a half beat.

"Tell me about the role of Andrew Jackson in *New Orleans*?" asked Will.

He seemed to wince at the very mention of the title. "It was a great role."

"Can you tell us how you got it?"

"Well, my agent, Noah Field, had a lot to do with it," he said generously.

Off to the side, Sue snorted in disgust, and Will shot her a quick reproving glance.

"Still, as I understand it, you first learned of the film on your own, and managed to secure a copy of the script privately. Only then did Mr. Field approach Precision Pictures on your behalf."

"That's true," he agreed with evident reluctance.

It was increasingly clear this was an exceptionally nice guy, uncomfortable badmouthing anyone; he'd have to grow a serious set of balls fast.

"It sounds like an unusual project, not very commercial. Why did you want to do it so badly?"

He hesitated. "I really can't say. I just loved the script."

"It wasn't only because it was a big career opportunity – the *subject* spoke to you in a deep and meaningful way."

There was a sudden glint of moisture in his eyes, and Will made sure the kid was getting it.

"I know this isn't easy, Mike...but it was then, shortly after you signed the contract, that this claim was made about you. That you had engaged in – forgive me, but this is the claim – that you'd engaged in, as they call it, hate speech."

"I never said it!" he said with sudden animation.

"I know that," said Will gently. "But that was the claim — that while you were working on *Cry Babeee, Cry!* you'd been overheard saying how much you love America."

He shook his head. "I never said it."

"...And it was further asserted that you'd been earlier heard to say that for all its faults, America is the greatest nation on earth."

"He's not stupid!" interrupted Sue.

"Evan, stop the camera!" He turned to her. "Do I look like I need your help?"

"I'm sorry. Maybe we believe that, but we'd *never* say it in front of people!"

"Okay," he allowed, letting her off the hook, and signaled Evan to resume shooting.

"Now, Michael, I want to get to Marc Guerin..."

He instantly tensed.

"Can you tell me what you think of him?"

"He's a very fine young actor. One of our best."

"You do not know him personally?"

He shook his head no. "I'm a great admirer of his work."

"So, obviously, you were excited at the prospect of co-starring with him in this picture..."

"Yes," he said softly.

"It must have hurt terribly, when these charges arose, these false accusations, when he turned on you so viciously. Without *any* evidence."

His eyes darted toward his wife, then back to his attorney. "It was...disappointing. But I really don't think it was personal."

"Guerin stabbed you in the back, Michael, you can say it!" he said in some exasperation. "What more can they do to you?"

"I just don't want to accuse anyone of anything," protested Sawyer.

Will was ready to drop it, it was clear he was *still* terrified of the repercussions. But after a long moment, Sawyer added, with inexpressible sadness, "I just don't want to do to anyone else what they've done to me."

Thank God, thought Will, he'd let the camera keep going. This was exactly the moment he'd been hoping for.

The dwarf lawyer was greatly heartened by the session with Sawyer.

No doubt about it, between the public sympathy the guy brought to the table and the appalling particulars of his case, he was shaping up as an excellent client. True enough, getting him out of this fix and salvaging his career wouldn't be easy. But through a deft mix of public relations, charm and menace, it might be doable, perhaps even without bringing suit, especially if his P.I. could dredge up with some potent stuff on his most deadly persecutor, Guerin, from whatever muck the star had slithered through on his crawl to the top.

At the same time, he already knew that wouldn't be enough. There were other attorneys, mere singles hitters, who might conceivably do the same (if maybe not as well, or with the same *élan*). What made Will unique in American jurisprudence was not only the fearlessness with which he took on the totalitarians, but that he always swung for the fences.

In this case, that meant exposing this new Hollywood blacklist itself for the moral monstrosity it was; indeed, as an implicit conspiracy in execution and consequences it was as reprehensible as its predecessor which, thanks to 40 years of books, movies and heartrending PBS specials, millions of

Americans earnestly believed had exacted a human toll surpassing the Spanish Inquisition.

In his hotel room, he had begun researching that earlier blacklist. Books were piled on every available surface, dozens of them, covering all aspects of those long-ago traumatic events; both general histories, and memoirs of those caught up in the maelstrom. He took special interest in those whose careers had been destroyed, including several members of the Hollywood Ten – writers and directors who had gone to prison for refusing to name other alleged Communists – as well as those of such lesser leftist luminaries as Gene Kelly's former wife, Betsy Blair. These were all unrepentant, and some, written years afterward, still bristled with anger. But, too, other accounts of the period were more nuanced and thoughtful, and a couple even had some laughs. Will especially enjoyed a volume called *Tender Comrades*, a range of reminiscences of those who'd survived that difficult long-ago time, many flashing perspective and good humor.

The dwarf attorney may have ideologically been as far from these people as you could get, and he was certainly no sentimentalist, but he was scrupulously fair-minded, and a warrior for individual rights, and there was no question that in almost every instance, these had been cavalierly tossed aside.

Yet what he found of greatest interest, because these were of the greatest potential use, were the accounts of how the blacklist had been defeated, exposed for the pernicious thing it was, and tossed into the ashbin of history. For even then there had been some with the balls – and, like Kirk Douglas and the director Otto Preminger, the standing – to finally hire those who'd hitherto been rendered unhireable.

Too, he ran across a figure he'd never heard of, but whose story he found especially compelling: John Henry Faulk, a folksy storyteller who, having enjoyed some success on early television before losing his career to the blacklist, took his tormentors to court. It was a long and tortuous process, detailed in Faulk's memoir *Fear On Trial*, but he eventually won his lawsuit, and in exposing the blacklisters to the light of day, helped end their reign of terror.

Inevitably, as he read, the germ of the idea that had been in the attorney's ever-active mind from the beginning took on fuller shape.

As his client, Michael Sawyer would be at the center of the case. But could it be any clearer that what had befallen Michael was compelling evidence of the threat faced by anyone working in this most vital of industries who risked deviating from approved wisdom so much as an iota on a vast range of subjects?

What better way to take on this new blacklist than to launch a class action on behalf of its targets?

Will figured finding potential plaintiffs would be the easiest part, since it was suspected there were a fair number of secret conservatives in the business (if perhaps not quite as many as there were secret Communists in the '40s). Indeed, even before leaving New York he'd heard rumors that the boldest among them sometimes met clandestinely, and he put out word that he was eager to attend such a gathering.

For a week he heard nothing, and was about to abandon the plan, but then got a late night call.

"Is this Will Tripp, the attorney?" asked a husky voiced woman.

"Who's asking?"

"A friend."

"I understand."

"8:45 sharp tomorrow morning. Corner of Chase and Langdon, down the street from your hotel. Make sure you're not followed."

She was off before he got a chance to ask if it was OK to bring along his team. But that was just as well, he intended to bring them anyway.

The next morning they were at the appointed spot, not knowing what to expect, when one of the detestable little Prius hybrids so ubiquitous in these parts drew up to the curb, an Uber placard prominently displayed on the dash. The middle-aged driver, mustached, balding and in knock-off Ray-Bans, got out.

He quickly scoped out the scene then, satisfied, approached Will. "Looks okay." He shot him a fleeting smile. "Sorry about the cloak and dagger stuff. Name's Phil."

The attorney nodded, as it hit him that most everyone in this town was a child playing pretend, "No problem, can't be too careful."

He started for the Prius, followed by the others.

"Not there," said Phil, "there."

He pointed at a green delivery van parked across the street, the words **SPARKLE CLEANERS** stenciled on the sides, its front windows blacked out.

Shepherding them to it, he threw open the back doors. "Make yourselves comfortable."

That wasn't going to happen. Once they'd laid the ramp for Marjorie's chair and they were all inside, Phil slammed the doors shut, and they were in darkness. In lieu of seats, Will and Arthur XXX sat on the hard benches lining the sides, as in prison wagons. The driver, behind a wall of metal, was unseen.

They rode in near-silence for half an hour, before the van turned from asphalt onto a gravel road, and ten minutes later it crunched to a half. The doors swung open and, eyes adjusting to the sudden brightness, Will felt himself lifted down by a pair of strong hands – Phil's.

They'd stopped before a secluded, much neglected, ranch-style house, a lone bedraggled palm drooping on a patch of yard gone to brown. The Prius, which they'd followed here, was parked ahead of the van.

Arthur XXX hopped from the van, and began setting down the ramp for Marjorie. But already Phil was motioning for Will to follow him into the house.

"We could only get five others on short notice…" he said.

"That's fine, that's a start."

"I should warn you, they're all pretty unsure about this."

Inside, the place, obviously long deserted, was musty, sparsely furnished, and reeked of disinfectant. As he followed Phil into a larger room in the back, its shades drawn, the dwarf attorney could dimly make out the others. Several sat in dilapidated soft chairs, but a couple were huddled in the corners, like refugees on an illicit ship. One of these had draped a blanket over his head.

"Okay, everyone," called Phil, with jarring good cheer, "as promised — Will Tripp, Esquire. A true light in the darkness."

"Just call me 'attorney for the damned,'" he said in kind. The title had once been Clarence Darrow's, but the comparison had occasionally been made, and Will figured it was there for the taking. "I can see I've come to the right place. As Darrow said, I stand on the thin line between good and American public opinion."

In the semi-darkness, one of the others laughed hoarsely, and the visitor acknowledged this with a nod. "Always great to be among friends."

"Everyone here…" began Phil "…we're part of a group. Friends of Frank — as in Sinatra."

"Ah," said Will vaguely, not getting the connection.

"FS – for Free Speech," explained the guy who'd laughed, as Will made note of his Brooklyn accent.

"Got it."

"Which is fuckin' *dead* in this town."

Clearly he was most brazen in the bunch, "You work in the business?"

"Twenty-three years." The hoarse laugh again. "I'm the most important guy on every set.'"

"Oh, yeah?"

"Pete's in…is it okay to say, Pete?"

"What the fuck, you already gave my name. Food services."

"He feeds the cast and crew."

"Did. No more."

"What happened?"

Pete exhaled loudly. "Didn't kneel."

"How's that?"

"We were setting up for a late night shoot on a piece of shit HBO series – the one about teenage nymphomaniacs…"

"The one Mike Sawyer was on…"

"No, a different one…And between takes, Monday Night Football is on, Cowboys-Saints. So as soon as they start the national anthem, everyone takes a knee."

"You mean the players, on TV…"

"No, there, on the set…On the sidewalk – they were shooting exteriors."

"But not you."

"Everyone else. Said I wasn't comfortable, said I had bad knees."

"Something like that, word gets around fast…" came another voice.

"Yeah, by next week, they'd brought on a new outfit."

"You've all had experiences like that?" asked Will. "You've all lost work?"

No one said anything.

"How about you, Todd," prompted Phil, the *de facto* host, "care to share?"

Will recoiled. He detested the phrase, belonging as it did to the vocabulary of ostentatious sensitivity. But this was not the time or place. "Please, I'm very interested," he offered encouragingly.

"Go on, Phil, you can tell," said Todd, as Will realized both that he was the one beneath the blanket, and almost surely gay. "I can't even say it, the whole subject makes me want to *puke.*"

"Okay." Phil turned to Will. "You'd definitely be familiar with Todd's work. You've done how many commercials…?"

"Oh, so many I lose track!"

"*National* brands!" chimed in one of the others, supportively.

"They always say I have that young husband *look,*" said Todd.

"But now his agent won't even send him out on calls." Phil paused, then, *sotto vocce*: "Wrong color."

Will made a mental note. Even here, this wasn't something comfortably spoken out loud.

"The last one I was up for," picked up Todd, from beneath the blanket, "was for Hellman's mayonnaise – and they actually told me I had it, before they changed their minds.

The agency said they had to have an interracial couple. So I said 'That's okay, it can be me and a black girl...'"

"Todd, shut up," came a sudden hiss from one of the others, who realized he was unaware that suddenly there was a huge black man looming in the doorway, pushing a woman in a wheelchair. Though Arthur was being careful not to scowl, he was wearing his work dashiki.

"Don't worry, they're with me," Will hurriedly assured. In fact, he had brought them along precisely because he wanted to show that, should they join him in this fight, for once they would have such allies in *their* corner. "I'm sorry, Todd, you were saying...?"

"Is it okay, is it safe...?"

"Absolutely," said Phil, "we've just been joined by a couple of Mr. Tripp's colleagues."

"Anyway, my agent said, no, they like it better with a black husband and white wife! And, by the way, she actually had the nerve to say to my face that she prefers that also – my own agent! Ask me, it's all these liberal white women at the ad agencies playing out their own little sexual fantasies."

There was another ominous silence – was this going *too* far? – before Arthur spoke up in annoyance. "I swear, watching commercials these days, you'd think there *are* no white couples in America."

Within a few minutes the rest were volunteering their tales. Doris, formerly a staff writer on a family sit-com, had made the mistake of using "partial birth abortion" instead of "IDX" (for intact dilation and extraction) within the hearing of a producer. Carl, a young sound engineer, was overheard mentioning he'd once served Jon Voight while working as a waiter, and he was "a nice guy." Dave, a longtime agent at one of the powerhouse firms, said he was usually so careful that in the last election cycle, he'd had a Biden sign on his front lawn and a Bernie sign on his roof, facing the studios. But then he'd been suspended and nearly fired after involuntarily recoiling at the sight of a biological woman attempting to use a urinal in the office men's room, "and now I'm a sitting duck."

Will took it all in with concern, and rising hope, and finally asked the question: Would they be willing to go public with such stories?

"There's a conspiracy of silence in this town," he said, carried along, as he often was, by the power of his own words, "and I say it's time to expose it!"

It was as if the temperature in the room dropped 50 degrees.

"There've gotta be hundreds of people in the same boat," he continued, "maybe thousands, and it's just wrong!"

Silence.

He glanced at Phil, who was staring at his feet. In desperation, he turned to Arthur for support.

"No justice, no peace," his colleague obliged with an upraised fist, and Will shook his head – not *that* one.

"We mmmmmust all hang together," Marjorie spoke up for the first time, "or asssssssu-redl-y....."

"…We'll all hang separately," Will hurriedly completed Franklin's timeless observation. "Well said!"

But already it was a lost cause. Moments later, watching them drift from the room, he realized he'd never so much as gotten any of their last names – or even necessarily their real first ones.

"It's actually pretty impressive," exclaimed Danny Valenzuela, "this *hijo de puta* Guerin came from *serious* poverty."

"Tell me something I don't know," replied Tripp. "I can also read Wikipedia."

Sitting before his MacBook Air in the kitchen in his Bronx apartment, Valenzuela smiled. The internet encyclopedia was a private joke between them. It was not just a fount of misinformation – invariably put there, as Will well knew, by the subjects' enemies, but shorthand for the half-assed effort so many bring to life's most elementary tasks.

"I mean, this time it's not just the usual P.R. bullshit," said the P.I. "Didn't go to school 'til he was nine — could hardly talk English, just Cajun gibberish. For supper he used to eat snakes and beetles and crap from the swamp."

"That helps them, not us..."

"Just saying..."

"And, by the way, ever taste snake meat? It's good."

"You haven't either, you little asshole."

"It's what I hear." He paused. "I know you got better than that."

Valenzuela laughed. After all this time working together, they read one another's minds. "Well, there is how he got started in the business." He paused a half beat before letting it drop. "Doing porn."

This definitely *was* of interest. Had he thought about it, which he never had, Will would have guessed he'd probably come into the business the usual way, playing small parts and then larger ones, until he broke out in the first entry of what would become the *Fast, Faster, Fastest* franchise. Though the picture starred fast cars and explosions as much as they did the stud newcomer with the mischievous grin playing wiseass Nick Storey, his future was assured.

In his hotel room a continent away, the attorney made a note on the pad by his side. "Tell me more. How hard core?"

"Better yet..."

Valenzuela turned his computer toward the door open to his living room, and clicked the TV remote. From across the country, Will saw the TV screen in the next room flicker to life.

Since it was just a 24-inch screen, and on the other side of the room, it took the attorney a moment to recognize what he was seeing: two nude women simultaneously working on a man lying spread eagle.

"Move closer, goddamn it!"

The picture jostled for a few seconds, as Valenzuela complied, but now his friend could pick up more detail. Guerin – and it definitely *was* Guerin, though a much younger version – with his hands bound to the bedposts.

"Picture's called *She'll Take It All,* he plays Mitch, the handyman."

He watched a moment. "Really crappy production values," observed Will, flashing his familiarity with the genre.

"Muted the sound. With all the shrieking and grunting it sounds like a barnyard." He paused. "Guerin went by Buck Bighorn in the credits. Just had this one scene, but the whole thing revolves around him. The handyman's known to the women of the town as 'The Cocksman.'"

"Can see why." He reflected a moment. "No small parts, just small actors. Probably didn't hurt when he got out to Hollywood."

The P.I. chuckled. "Love how your mind works."

"Hey, women in the film business have needs, just like school teachers." He paused. "How many of these did he do?"

"Far as I know, this one, and one other, *Come What May.* But I also want to check out the sequel, just to be sure — *Come Again, Big Boy.*"

"Absolutely, nail that down." If there was one thing the investigator never did, it was cut corners on research.

Valenzuela carried the computer back to the kitchen and reappeared on the screen.

"So where'd you learn this?"

"The Reid Cinema Archives, in Connecticut — they're like hoarders, an unbelievable amount of stuff on movie stars, they stash away whatever anyone sends them. They've got 50 boxes of random stuff on Guerin, completely unsorted!"

"I'm impressed…"

"You should be, I spent nearly a week living and breathing *este idiota.*"

Will's phone sounded with a ping.

"Take a read," said Valenzuela.

Opening the text, Will saw it was a photo of an article headlined: *PORN STUDIES 101.*

"Where's this from?"

"A college newspaper, believe it or not, from 2003. Place called Buchanan College in Pennsylvania. Our boy was the big attraction at an 'erotic film festival' they put on there."

"Buchanan College? Never heard of it."

"Amazing, isn't it. Paper's called *The Buchanan Buccaneer.* Only a couple of other articles anywhere even mentioned the porn stuff, and this was the only one that gets into any detail. The P.R. people totally buried it…"

"And the lapdogs in the media."

Valenzuela snorted. "Tell me about it, *hijo.* Just spent days wading through every 'profile' in *Vanity Fair, People* and *The New York* fucking *Time*s."

"Looks like this one actually has some reporting…" said Will, scanning the article.

"Right. At the time Guerin was so hard up for publicity, he spilled his guts to this idiot kid."

Will smiled. One thing he admired about Danny was that his judgments of the talentless and self-deluded were almost as harsh as his own. "Thought you said he was a good reporter."

"I mean at least he asked some questions. And, I'll give him this, he knew his dirty movies. But his writing – *Analfabeto!*"

"Help me out."

"Illiterate! I tell you, little man, you read a thing like this and weep for American education."

Scrolling down, the attorney saw the article was fairly long, 800 or a thousand words. "Looks like he talks quite a bit about his background..."

"It's all there — drunk father, in and out of the house, slutty mother...the other losers he ran with."

"How old you say Guerin was when he talked to this guy?"

"Seventeen."

"Amazing, and today the guy's a world-class..." he paused, chuckled, "...prick. But it does sound like he had it pretty rough."

"Does." Agreed Valenzuela. "Then, again..."

"What?"

"That's what he wanted you to think — even then, doing dick films, he was playing the sensitive, wounded artist."

"And he's not?"

The P.I. hesitated. He was far from a psychologist, in fact, thought most of it was crap, but he'd spent the past week all but living in Marc Guerin's head. "This guy was never a victim. What he is is a survivor, *un camaleon*, he always puts out the version of himself that's most useful at the moment."

On his pad, Will jotted down the word "chameleon," in English, then, misspelled, in Spanish.

"Look at the part I underlined near the bottom, where he brags about the stuff him and his boys got away with..."

"Right," said the attorney, scrolling down. "Got it!"

"He called them 'My real family,' and he meant it."

Will found the reference, and read that paragraph closely, then the one after. "Good work," he said, as close as he ever came to a compliment. "So I guess next…"

"Way ahead of you, little man!" the P.I. cut him off. "Heading down to Louisiana tomorrow."

"I really can't get over it!" exclaimed Will, of his experience with the Friends of Frank. "I mean, Christ, *these* are our allies?! What a bunch of pansies!"

Beside him, his companion smiled wistfully. "Maybe – but that's not to say they were wrong." He paused. "They're trying to survive in this business, you're not."

At 96, Jack Berke was a wonder; not just among the oldest residents of The Motion Picture and Television Country House, but without a doubt the sharpest. Indeed, half an hour earlier, on arriving for their appointment and being directed to the figure on the bench alongside the community center, Will thought there'd been a mix-up. Trim in jeans and a windbreaker, his head still full and only partially gone to grey, the guy might've passed for 60. When he got close, Will saw he was working on last week's *New York Times'* Sunday crossword.

"Mr. Berke?"

Berke looked up. "Ah, the celebrated Mr. Tripp, I've been looking forward to this."

"Same here, sir," he replied. "Glad you could see me."

This was more than mere courtesy. A Brooklyn-born screenwriter of some note in the '50s and '60s – *Desperation*

Central with Robert Mitchum was among his credits – Berke was one of the few still around who'd experienced, in fact, been enmeshed in, the original blacklist. The dwarf attorney deemed his perspective of potentially great importance – as eventually, perhaps, would be his testimony. Berke had even written a number of times about that period.

"If you'll forgive me," he said now, indicating the magazine, "I'd just like a moment to finish this, so then I can give you my full attention."

"Of course."

Turning back to his puzzle, he chuckled. "A bad old habit. But it's the only thing in this piece of shit newspaper still worth a damn."

Will laughed, delighted as much by the old guy's ready vulgarity as by his take on *The Times*. "Take your time," he said, even as he noted with resignation that he'd only just started.

So he was further astonished to see him whip through the puzzle in ten minutes, filling in the spaces, in ink, without even momentary pause.

"Now, then," said Berke, turning to him, "how can I be of service?"

The old man listened with keen interest as the attorney explained about Sawyer, and how he'd come to take on the Sawyer case; then moved onto his frustration with others he'd hoped might help draw attention to the rampant suppression of opinion in Hollywood.

"The fact is, I'd be surprised if you could find a dozen people in this town who'd put their necks on the line," observed Berke, when he finished. The money's pretty good out here – IF you're working."

"I get that. Of course. Still, I was hoping maybe I could get just a couple who'd…"

"It was always that way. Christ, what the hell is it you think got *me* out here? The telegram Herman Mankiewicz sent to his buddy Ben Hecht back East – 'Millions are to be grabbed out here, and your only competition is idiots. Don't let this get around.'" He laughed heartily. "Liked the sound of that – nothing wrong with wanting to be a writer *and* rich."

But he knew the little man beside him expected more; and, in fact, he expected more of himself. "Listen," he said, turning serious, "this business tests you, it makes you find out who you are fast. And probably, if you're honest, you're an asshole."

"In other words, basically nothing's changed," came back Will in frustration. "It's the same now as then. Except now no one calls it a blacklist!"

"Actually, no," he said without hesitation, "there are a lot of differences."

The dwarf lawyer leaned in closer. In a world overwhelmingly populated by the moronic and the gullible, it was exceedingly rare for him to defer to the wisdom of another. But there was something about this guy…

"I was young and stupid," he began describing his own hard-earned experience, "19, and arriving at UCLA on the GI Bill fresh from Okinawa. Remember, we were still friends with Russia then, it was easy to get swept up in all the idealistic prattle about peace, and cooperation and" – he chuckled – "and how America was the problem. I was never a Red, but I was pretty damn close."

When the crackdown came, he said, the only reason he wasn't blacklisted was he wasn't important enough to notice. "My only credit was for a few scenes on a B-western for Republic; my failure was my get-out've-jail-free-card."

But others, including close friends, were not so lucky. "They were good people, idealistic, just misguided, and they got caught in the net."

Will nodded. "That's what I've always heard."

"Yes, well here's something you don't, at least not often, long as I'm filling in the blanks. "Some they went after, including some that afterward got to be thought of as big heroes, really were bad hombres."

"You mean they were Communists."

"Shit, most of those who joined the Party were just soft-headed dupes, like me. No, I'm talking dangerous. Straight-up Stalinist totalitarians. The sort that, if they'd ever gotten to run things, like they planned, they'd've lined you and me up against a wall without a second thought."

"Sounds like today," snorted Will, only half joking.

"Does, doesn't it?"

The old man fell silent, looking over the lawn toward Mulholland Drive.

"You were going to tell me about the difference."

"Well, like I say, there were also a lot of good people who got named, some of them were destroyed. For a while you could taste the fear, it felt like it could happen to just about anyone." He paused. "At the same time – how do I put this? – most everyone, in the business and out, no matter what side they were on, would tell you in private the blacklist was a shameful thing. It made everyone felt dirty. And when it ended, even the studio suits who'd enforced it were relieved. But now, people out here today..."

His voice trailed off, and the attorney completed the thought. "They're *proud* of it."

"Exactly. They think they're doing the Lord's work, or would if they didn't sneer at religion. They have no doubt they're fighting *evil.*"

While this was not precisely news, Will had never heard it expressed so clearly. "There doesn't have to be a formal blacklist, it's a blacklist by common consent."

Berke chuckled. "A blacklist without the list – though I have no doubt many of them have found the membership lists of the NRA or the Republican Party useful. The line they always give is how it's important to work with people who 'share your values.'"

"So much for diversity."

"Wrong kind." He smiled mirthlessly. "For me, the work started drying up in the '70s..."

"In the '70s?"

"...after I contributed to *Governor* Reagan." He shook his head. "The 'New Hollywood' they were calling it, *Easy Rider* and all that. The lefties were back throwing their weight around."

"And now..." The old man paused again, then continued, not with acrimony, but as a simple statement of fact: "well, the Stalinists have won, haven't they? They run everything. What gets on TV and in the movies, and on the news' broadcasts; what you're allowed to hear and say and think. Straight up totalitarians, and they spread their poison to every corner of the country."

"Like your optimism," he observed with a laugh, though of course no one lived that reality more fully than he did.

"Well, it's no longer my problem, is it?" said Berke. "If I gotta check out, this isn't a bad time." He paused. "I know you didn't come here for advice, here's some anyway."

"Whatever you got."

"Don't think you can change the way things are out here, it's too big a job. It'll be hard enough saving that miserable sonvabitch client of yours."

Will nodded.

"Remember, you're dealing with people so full of their own virtue, they genuinely have no idea how mean spirited they are. You start to think they're incapable of embarrassment."

"But..." encouraged Will, gesturing with his tiny hand for him to complete the thought.

"I think about something Bob Mitchum once told me — that the only difference between him and every other star was that he'd actually done serious time behind bars." He looked down into the other's eyes. "Trust me, look hard enough and there's something to be gotten on every damn one of them — tax evasion, sexual assault, perjury, extortion, Christ knows what." He paused, on the remote chance the lawyer hadn't already fully absorbed the message. "That kind of information's a sledgehammer, it gets things done."

He had no need to worry, his companion had already been thinking along the same lines.

Forty minutes after landing at Lafayette Regional Airport, Danny Valenzuela pulled up in his Ford Taurus rental before The Cajun Corners Motel in Fleuret. It was the P.I.'s custom to go for local color, and this establishment had it in spades. Located in the midst of mini-malls, car dealerships and fast food joints, it was a piece of classic '50s kitsch that had somehow survived more or less intact, its vintage neon sign crackling on and off even in the bright late morning sunshine.

When he entered, the heavyset young woman in stretch pants behind the counter looked up from the soap opera she'd been watching on a pre-flat screen TV.

The sign out front said $45 a night, but when he offered cash in advance, she readily agreed to a weekly rate of two fifty.

He didn't have to, but the P.I. was always looking to save Marty Katz money.

"You here on business, or what?"

"Uh uh, just had some time and always heard it was an interesting part of the world."

Taking the key, he'd started up the nearby stairway, when he turned back. "Excuse me?"

"Yessir."

"About how long will it take me to get to Julien?"

"Lookin' to visit Marc Guerin's hometown?"

"Figured I'd have a look."

"Maybe an hour an' a half. Not much to see there, though."

Entering his room, he set down his bag on the creaky bed, took off his jacket and shirt, and shaved – no hot water, just lukewarm – then put on a fresh shirt. Before leaving, standing at the door, he took a long moment to look over the section he'd underlined from a piece in the *Buchanan Buccaneer*:

> *Buck told me he had such a hard childhood growing up that he is grateful and happy to have the work he does now in erotic cinema. He says in comparison to such a childhood, the long hours before the camera are "like a vacation" and "a piece of cake." He told me he was often on his own as a boy, since his parents were not in his life very much, and he had to live by his wits.*

Danny paused, once again shuddering at the awfulness of the prose.

> *He said that the main thing that saved him was being with troubled other boys in similar circumstances. "There were four of us, and we all had different nicknames, such as Tiny, Bayou and Yoda. I was called Little Man, since I was the youngest, only thirteen." He adds, "you could say they were my real*

family." However, he also adds that at times they got in serious trouble, and he was personally fortunate he did not wind up in jail. "Yes, we did some pretty bad s____t," adds The Cocksman with a laugh, including robbery and breaking and entering among their various "hijinx."

Fortunately for us viewers of his films, we are getting the benefit today of his "life experiences," since Buck "The Cocksman" Bighorn, says he puts the feelings derived from such experiences in his acting on the screen today."

Guerin's "life experiences" – Valenzuela chuckled at the phrase – that's what he was after. In detail. The dwarf lawyer couldn't have been more clear about what he needed: enough damning information to not just bring the bastard down, but make him an object lesson for all those who'd destroy others for the crime of independent thought.

It was no easy assignment, especially not here, in Guerin's backyard, where he was revered – and was sure to be protected – as a secular god. But closing the door behind him and starting down the stairs, the P.I. was still smiling.

"I'm hurt," said Noah Field, "I thought I'd be your first call!"

"Well, you know," said Will, taken aback, "I wanted to get the lay of the land first." He paused. "So I'm guessing you know what this is about."

"Of course, and I want you to know I'm there for you. I'll do anything I can."

Pleased as he was, the dwarf lawyer was surprised; and, after what he'd been hearing from the Sawyers, more than a little dubious. "That's great to hear, I'll definitely take you up on it."

"Mike Sawyer's not just a client, he's a dear friend."

"Right, I know he and Sue feel the same way."

Will glanced down at the page Cheryl had prepared on the agent. She'd set one line in bold: **He is said to have in abundance the single quality most essential to his work: he's incapable of embarrassment.**

Still, Will considered Fields' cooperation essential. As Sawyer's agent, he'd negotiated the disputed contracts on his behalf. Moreover, while he was still feeling his way, Field could be his conduit to the industry heavyweights he needed to see, if only to probe for their weaknesses.

Including, and especially, Marc Guerin himself.

"So when can we get together?" he asked

"When would I like to? Yesterday!" the agent laughed. "See how eager I am."

Fleetingly the dwarf lawyer wondered if out here even the most obvious jokes had to be identified as such. "How about tomorrow?"

"How about *today?*" Field one-upped him. "Let's do lunch!"

Will glanced at the time on his phone. "It's 4:09."

"Fine, call it dinner – I'm doing intermittent fasting, it all smooshes together."

"Sounds good. Where?"

"I'll have my assistant give you a call with the details." He paused, then added, with disarming sincerity. "I want to tell you something, Will, even before we meet…"

"Okay."

"May I call you Will? Because I hear you sometimes have a problem with that…"

"You have good sources, I'm impressed."

"No, *I'm* impressed – that's what I want to say. Impressed and excited. I'm a great admirer, I've been following you for a long time."

As he headed due south from Lafayette into the heart of bayou country, Danny was struck by its desolation and savage beauty. The Atchafalaya Basin seemed out of the time of the dinosaurs: flat as Kansas, with water everywhere, yet oddly menacing. Turning off Route 49 onto a two-lane byway, he was wholly lost to civilization, twisted trees rising from the muck on either side, brilliant colored birds making noises like those in the jungle films he'd watched as a kid. Several times, fascinated, he drew to the side of the road, just to marvel.

Now and then, in the midst of the endless swamp, he came upon a town, most with French-sounding names, and so tiny they were over before they began; as well as an occasional roadside shack selling crawfish, andouille, alligator or other local delicacies. The sense of finding himself in another world was heightened by the mundane act of switching on the radio and finding a Cajun station, the driving accordion and fiddle providing a joyous counterpoint to the singer's strange, mournful wail.

Man, I tell ya, il fait beautiful, aujourd'hui, the weatherman exclaimed of the near perfect day, and Danny couldn't agree more.

There was little to distinguish Julien from the other towns in the area; a half dozen streets of mainly cinderblock houses clustered around a bleak commercial strip, with a McDonald's at the end, and a sprawling trailer park beyond.

Nothing but the small sign adjacent to the town's only stoplight: Birthplace of Marc Guerin.

Pulling to the side of the deserted main drag, Danny lowered his window.

"Excuse me," he called to an elderly black man laboriously making his way on foot toward the McDonald's, "the police station close by?"

Unexpectedly, the man shot him a smile, showing gums nearly devoid of teeth, as he pointed. "Too near. Jus' 'round there."

Sure enough, turning the corner there was a small red brick structure grandly proclaiming, in large embossed silver letters, MUNICIPAL BUILDING.

He'd just parked across the street when two uniformed cops emerged. He recognized the older one as the man he was looking for: Chief Fred Borden.

He watched them stroll down three doors and turn into a small restaurant, the sign outside doing double duty as the name of the place and its menu: REAL CAJUN COOKING.

After a couple of minutes, he followed, entering through a screen door. As his eyes adjusted to the dim light, he was hit by a smell so strong he could taste it – a mix of whatever was cooking and a thousand years of stale cigarette smoke.

There were four cheesecloth-covered tables, only the one with the cops occupied.

"Jus' you?" called the woman behind the Formica counter.

"Just me."

"Well, go on then, sit down."

He took the table next to the cops.

"You from out've state?" asked the chief, pleasantly, as soon as he did.

He smiled. "Pretty obvious, huh?"

"Son, anyone within a hunerd miles a here, chances are I arrested 'em one time or t'other."

Danny laughed; this was going to be easier than he thought. "You're Chief Borden, I recognize you from your clippings."

Borden positively lit up. "You come out here lookin' for me?"

"Actually, yeah. And to take a look at the town." He offered his hand, and the other took it. "Rich Hernandez." The same name he'd used at the motel.

"Where you from, son?"

He was pretty sure he didn't mean the locale. "*The New York Post*. Long as I was visiting down here, they asked if maybe I could do a Sunday feature on Marc."

"So you freelance?" asked the chief, showing off his understanding of how these things worked.

"That's right. Do stuff for them from time to time – usually about soccer."

Oddly enough, this was true; the Mexican-born Valenzuela was passionate about the game. And it was also true, and more to the point, that at the scrappy tabloid, foe of all things *New York Times*, he had a friend who would vouch for him, if it came to that.

"You hear that, Breaux?" Borden exclaimed to the other, "he come all the way from New York to see us." He turned back to the visitor. "This here is Corporal Breaux."

The proprietor set a heaping platter of the local delicacy on the table between them.

"You like crawfish, son?"

"Never ever had 'em."

"Well, then, you're in for a treat. Look here,"

Taking up one of the small crustaceans between his thumb and forefinger, he demonstrated how to get at the morsel of meat; straightening it out, then pinching its curved tail.

"Here you go."

Danny took the bit of flesh from the chief and popped it into his mouth. "Wow! Delicious!" He turned to the waitress. "Miss, same for me, please!"

"See that?" said the chief, pleased. "You know, over the years I must've talked to 20 people like you about Marc."

"I can believe it, I've read the clips."

"He's the best thing that ever happened to Julien, Marc Guerin is!"

"He's one helluva an actor!"

"He's that, and more! He's one guy that never forgot where he came from." He leaned forward, and added. "You got good timin', I got an exclusive for you."

"Really?"

"We're gonna put up a permanent exhibition on Marc, it's gonna have some of his actual costumes."

Rich got his notebook. "I can use that? It's official?"

The other nodded. "It's an exclusive," he repeated, "no one else knows that!"

"Thank you!" Danny beamed at this unexpected bounty. "So what can you tell me about what he was like – when he was a kid, I mean."

"Oh, he was always a good kid. Maybe a little rough around the edges, but hard to find a kid around here that ain't."

Danny nodded. "Right, I've read that. Any specifics? Anything he did that stands out?"

"Well, he always got along pretty good with the girls and whatnot, I'll say that, and the other way around."

"Still does," agreed Danny with a chuckle.

"What I'd give!" Breaux spoke up for the first time.

"Oh, man, who wouldn't!" agreed Danny. He paused. "I read where Marc said he and his friends used to get a little rowdy."

"Well, I guess they did, can't blame kids for that."

"You recall any time in particular?"

The chief paused, a crawfish inches from his mouth. "Not really." He popped it in. "Just the usual sorts've stuff. Boys bein' boys. 'Youthful shenanigans' I s'pose you'd call it."

"Thanks," said Valenzuela, knowing not to press further. "Terrific stuff."

The waitress set down his platter "Okay if I quote that?"

"No problem, always happy to help."

"And maybe I can also get a shot of you outside headquarters?"

"Whatever you need!"

Danny picked up a crawfish, demonstrating his technique. "Like this?"

"Not quite," Both cops laughed. "But it's your first try, keep at it."

"By the way, happen to know if any of his old buddies are still around?"

He didn't even hesitate. "Oh, yeah, Kevin Broussard. He's down by St. Martinville. Him and Marc was real tight."

"Excellent choice," said Will, sliding into a back booth at the venerable Beverly Hills steak joint, The Palm. "I get the idea most restaurants in this town don't even know how to make a good fire."

Noah Field smiled engagingly. "Thought you'd like it. Like you say, I do my research."

The agent was pretty much as he appeared in the photos Cheryl had included, though, in a Dolce and Gabbana suit and remarkably good hairpiece, perhaps a bit younger looking than his 47 years. Although he owned a Porsche Carrera and a Tesla Model S, he'd arrived at the restaurant in a 2019 black Mercedes S550 – a respectable standard mid-level industry ride, but hardly flashy enough to show up anyone more powerful.

Field lingered momentarily before sitting down, checking something on his phone.

"Sorry," he said, putting it away, "don't mean to be rude, I'm in the middle of something important."

"No problem," replied Will graciously, "I'm used to dealing with assholes."

The agent laughed, delighted. "Touché!" Field laughed again, even louder. "Just great!"

"I mean it."

"I know you do. It's like I was telling you! And you're just what I hoped. This is gonna be fun!" He exhaled deeply, savoring the moment. "Anyway," he picked up, "like I say, the strip steak here is the best in town. Take my word for it."

"You come here a lot?"

"Only with special people. Other people, vegans, they'd kill me if they knew. Literally." He beamed. "Truly, Will, can't tell you how delighted I was to hear from you. Christ, moment I heard you were out here, I wanted to call you — you were at the top of my list."

Will nodded. "Well, I was glad to hear we're on the same page." He caught the other's momentary confusion. "About Michael Sawyer."

"Right, Michael," said Field. "Great guy. He's not just a client, he's a dear friend."

"Yes." Will paused. "What they're doing to him is a disgrace."

"Couldn't agree more," he said gravely. "An absolute disgrace."

The waiter appeared. "Excuse me, don't mean to interrupt. I'm Brian, I'll be your waitperson."

"Hello, Brian!" exclaimed the agent, brightly.

"How are you gentlemen this evening?"

"Fifteen percent better than perfect!"

"They're all actors here," he confided as Brian departed with their order, "or else aspiring Tarantinos. Others may disagree, but I say it never hurts to treat them like human beings. Just in case."

"Yeah, well I was gonna tell him to grow a pair and say 'waiter.'"

The agent again erupted in laughter. "Great! Just what I hoped." He dropped his voice. "But you never know, could be trans, don't want to go out on a limb."

Will's heart sank. "But we were talking about Michael."

"Yes, well…" Field hesitated. "He's a terrific talent, I've represented him a long time…"

"Will nodded. "So I understand."

"Don't quote me on this, I'm a big supporter of human rights and all, but I wish he hadn't said it."

"He says he didn't."

"Even so. People have very strong, passionate feelings…"

"Uh huh."

"Good people. On both sides. *All* sides. To me it's all so unnecessary." He paused. "Don't quote me on that."

"As his agent, I assumed you'd be his greatest defender."

"I am! Absolutely! Always!"

"Good, so we can *definitely* count on you, then?"

"You mean on the contract stuff?"

"That. And maybe helping out with some other things. There are some people I'm hoping you might put me in touch with."

He paused, seeming to weigh this. "Don't quote me on this, but the contract's a blind alley."

"It seems pretty straightforward to me."

"You don't want to go there." He stopped, then added meaningfully, "There's the morality clause." When Will continued staring at him blankly, he added in a whisper. "Hate speech."

Will almost laughed out loud. "That's a fight I'd *welcome!*"

Field sat back in his chair, as close to flabbergasted as he ever allowed himself to show; the magic phrase ordinarily ended every argument. But instantaneously, he recovered. "But how about if I ask you something?" he said, leaning forward conspiratorially.

"Excuse me?"

"Ever given any thought to getting involved in this business?"

"Show business?" said Will, taken aback.

"Because you're a natural."

The truth? Of course he had; who hadn't? "Screw that!"

"You're a born showman. And one of a kind. Who you are, the kinds of cases you do…"

"That's not why we're here."

"Speak for yourself." He laughed. "Listen, Will, this isn't a new thought, I've been following you a long time."

Despite himself, Will was flattered. It was true, few were so drawn to the big stage, or performed on it with such ease. The idea did have a certain seductive appeal.

"Look," pressed the agent, "I understand you're out here to do a job, Mike's your number one priority, I respect that, he's mine, too."

Will acknowledged the lie with a curt nod.

"We're not talking conflict of interest here."

"Good, glad to hear it."

"But know who I think about when I read about you, your cases, your *life?*" the agent pressed his advantage. "Clarence Darrow!"

Will nodded, but his eyes betrayed his interest – either this guy was very good, or very lucky.

"You know what Darrow once said?" Field pressed his advantage. "He said 'I never killed a man, but I read obituaries all the time with pleasure.' Is that you, or what?"

"*Plus* a dwarf," pointed out Will.

"Yes! And that's key!" he leaned even further across the table. "Don't quote me on this, but you could get away with anything! Stuff they'd never tolerate from anyone else, all the anti-PC shit! These teacher cases – imagine an HBO series where that was an episode. Showing all the sex! But in the interest of *justice!*"

"I'd have guessed people out here would all be on the other side on the teacher cases."

"Come on," scoffed the agent, "hot is hot – there's reality and there's bullshit!"

"Biological reality," agreed the attorney. "That was the whole basis of my defense."

"See, that's what you are, a fucking *truth teller*! That's gold in this business!"

"I do like that Darrow line," allowed Will.

"Sure, he gave great quote, like you. First heard it when I was I trying to get a project on him off the ground."

"Ahh."

"Tough sell, history. What you get is, *'who gives a fuck?'*
And I gotta admit, they have a point."

"I love history."

"Hey, I'm not arguing. I got a writer with a project
right now – fabulous, a true story. You heard of John D.
Rockefeller?"

"*Have I heard of John D. Rockefeller?*"

"I mean, yeah, people know he was a rich guy. But do
you know how he made his money…?"

"Oil," shot back Will.

"Wow, I can see you really do know your history…" He
paused. "Anyway, turns out his old man was a rapist."

"Rockefeller's father?"

The agent nodded, pleased. "*William* Rockefeller. So —
this is in the treatment — when the law goes after him, he
deserts the wife and kids, takes a new name, and has a new
family out West – he's also a bigamist. But later, when the
kid makes all the dough, the newspapers get wind of it, and
there's a big nationwide hunt for the old bastard. Yet, get this,
the son protects him. Why? Cause all these years later they've
gotten back together and forged a bond." He paused, before
the summing up he'd used in a dozen pitch meetings. "See,
that's the thing: they're *both* criminals, just in different ways.
Anti-heroes, with redeeming qualities. And you also got that
father-son thing going. And the anti-capitalism message,
which they *love*."

His companion stared at him blankly, suppressing his disgust.

"*Great,* right? But no sale. Why? Period piece, costs up the wazoo." He shook his head in frustration. "It's always the same thing: sure, now get me Tom Hanks for John D. Or Bradley Cooper. Or Marc Guerin."

Will was surprised by his sheer…matter-of-factness. "So you'd have no problem working with Guerin?" he asked.

The agent waited for the other to smile; no one couldn't possibly be so naïve. "Fuck, no! Who do I have to screw to make it happen?"

"Even after what he did to your pal Sawyer. That's just" – he snapped his fingers – "forgotten?"

Sensing the contempt, the agent readily nodded his understanding. "Look, I hear you. You're right. But you're not talking to King Solomon here, all right, or…" he hesitated. "Judge Judy. It's *not* forgotten, of course not, *ever,* just temporarily…set aside." He paused. "You know Guerin grossed over a billion last year in China alone?"

"*China?*" It had been a while since he'd heard anyone speak of the world's most menacing totalitarian regime without at least passing acknowledgement of the fact.

"Exactly, over a billion, *just* in China! Do the math – Marc Guerin signs onto your project and it gets done!"

"So no consequence…"

Field, too, was at a loss. Why was this little guy, smart as he was, having so much trouble with this?

But, too, he was annoyed with himself. Why the hell had he dropped the earlier thread when it had started to look so promising?

"But, you know," he said, "even this, right here, it's great stuff! It's exactly what the audience will love about the show — how fucking *principled* you are!"

"Yeah, well, appreciate it, but I'm out here to do a job, I can't wear two hats."

"Why not?"

"It's not ethical."

"You serious? — no one really thinks that way." He paused. "It could be it a plot point in an episode, a dilemma, you having to do both things at once. And you'd pull it off! Why, because you're fucking Will Tripp, that's why!"

"How come you curse so much?" He'd almost said "so *fucking* much," it was catching.

"It's the *lingua franca* out here. That means…"

"I know what it means…"

"Of course you do, you're Will fucking Tripp!"

"…and you're misusing it. Why not just say you've got no class?"

"I don't need a goddamn treatment," pressed the agent, "just give me a few lines on your best cases, the ones with curb appeal."

Brian appeared with their food, and set down the plates.

No question, it was unorthodox, reflected the dwarf attorney. Then, again, when in his career had he ever been anything but?

"Let me ask you something," he said as the waiter walked off. "Can you get me to Marc Guerin?"

The agent sipped his water before responding. "That's shooting pretty high – Guerin's not just a star, he's a fucking conglomerate, you have to work through his people…"

"So the answer is no."

"The answer is yes, in time…" — he smiled, shamelessly — "if you were a client."

This guy was good, no doubt about it; from the start, this whole thing had been a negotiation.

"Nothing on paper," said Will. "No commitment 'til you deliver."

"Done," replied the agent. "Just don't quote me on that."

Danny Valenzuela was waiting outside REAL CAJUN COOKING when the mud-spattered red Dodge pickup turned the corner and parked across the street.

Kevin Broussard, got out and slammed the door behind him, "You gotta be Hernandez," he called, "ain't no one else loiters in this damn town 'less he got a beer in his hand."

Danny laughed, liking the guy already. In faded coveralls and work boots, handsome face weathered, he could've been Marc Guerin's downhome older brother; and like Guerin's screen persona, he radiated the sense of being wholly at ease with himself.

"Don't mind the stink," he added, hand outthrust, "just got outta the swamp."

"No problem," said Danny, clasping it, "glad you could come."

Within a minute of entering the restaurant, Danny was made to understand he wasn't likely to get much new today. "I enjoy talkin' to you fellas well enough," said Broussard good naturedly, "but I done it so much by now, I'm kinda talked out." He laughed. "Should at least be gettin' paid by now."

"You're right — lunch is on me."

"So this is for a paper up in New York?"

"Yep – *The New York Post*."

"I been there once, New York. So, Rich, what's your angle?"

"My angle?" He hadn't anticipated such a question. "Well, I guess – no offense intended – how the world's biggest star came out of a place like this."

"None taken." He paused. "Yeah, we're pretty backward here — ain't got toilets or 'lectricty or nothin'."

"No, that isn't what I…"

"Jus' pullin' your chain." He smiled to show he meant it. "No, it's true, ain't much 'round here, most people get out soon as they find an excuse."

"How come you're still here?"

"Hell, I got out, too. Joined up with the Marines at 19, an' after that worked on an oil rig in the Gulf. Even lived in The Big Easy for a while, as a bouncer on Bourbon Street." He shrugged. "But I came back, started workin' the bayou. Turned out I liked rats more'n people."

Danny nodded; Chief Borden had mentioned Broussard was a trapper, selling his nutria pelts to buyers in New Orleans.

"No bullshit with swamp rats, never pretend to be better'n they are."

They were momentarily interrupted by the waitress, and Danny ordered crawfish and Kevin, "the usual."

"Must be tough work, trapping," the P.I. said.

"Oh, there's tougher. The Lord blessed nutria with thin sculls. Try takin' a club an' puttin' an *otter* out've its misery."

"Right, suppose so…"

He laughed. "Love talkin' to you city boys – could've said the other way 'round an' you wouldn't've known the difference."

"You're right."

The waitress returned with their order – "the usual" turned out to be a slab of American cheese between two slices of Wonder bread.

Danny picked up a crayfish and, demonstrating his newfound skill, squeezed the tail and the meat popped into his mouth.

"Not bad," observed Kevin.

"Thanks."

"Course, I wouldn't touch one myself – not after I seen a bucketload, all writin' and slimy, getting pulled from a sewer full of shit."

He smiled as his companion pushed the plate toward the center of the table.

"No, no, enjoy, jus' pullin' your chain."

"Anyway, tell me about Marc back then."

"Well, like everyone knows, he had it rough. Even rougher n' me. I had no mom or dad, so got farmed out to relatives, he was stuck with the ones he had. So a bunch of us useta hang together."

Danny nodded. "I've read about that. I read you were a really tight group, and Marc was kind've the baby."

"Yeah. More like the mascot, really." He smiled. "He was always a good kid, I'll tell ya that much. Maybe a little wild, but who wasn't?"

"Tell me about that. You ever get in trouble?"

"Coulda been worse. I got caught swipin' stuff couple've times. Once they got me takin' steaks out've the Piggly Wiggly up by New Iberia."

"How about Marc?"

He shook his head. "Nothin' like that. He kept his nose clean."

"He have a nickname?" he posed the question without apparent guile.

"What do you mean?" he asked with sudden wariness. "How come you ask me somethin' like that?"

"I read somewhere you all had nicknames for each other."

"Nobody ever asked me anythin' like that before. Like what?"

"Oh, lemme see." He pulled his pad from his jacket pocket and read. "Yoda. Bayou. Tiny." He looked up, quickly enough to see Broussard betrayed by eyes widened in surprise.

"Oh, that was nothin'," he said, "jus' us kiddin' around."

"So I'm guessing you would've been Bayou…"

"Can't even remember," he said, with a sudden hostile edge. "Don't know why you'd even ask about somethin' like that."

Danny nodded. "No big deal, just something I ran across."

"It was a long time ago, man, nobody cares about that stuff."

"Of course, understood." He gave Bayou his most engaging smile. "Probably won't even use it."

"Why, hello, HELLO!" exclaimed Noah Field, his voice so loaded with good cheer that Will heard his smile on the other end of the line. "I was getting worried, I wasn't sure I'd hear from you."

"We talked just yesterday."

"Feels like a century, that's how much I…"

"I think you knew you would."

The agent laughed. "Why's that?

"We're both in the business of reading people."

"True enough…so what do you say, Mr. Tripp?"

"Will."

"Excellente, so you're in!"

The dwarf attorney found the other's enthusiasm grating. "I think it's bullshit, but I'll give it a shot."

"Fantastic! You won't regret it."

"I regret it already."

"Just GREAT!" Field's laugh was so loud Will had to move the phone from his ear. "I tell you, you're a NATURAL."

"Just a shot. No commitment."

"When can you come by here? I need to see you yesterday!"

Talent Without Borders' Beverly Hills offices occupied the 20th and 21st floors of a gleaming glass tower on Wilshire's 9000 block. Field decided he would actually greet his new client personally in the lobby. Given that this was the town's most powerful agency and Field was a leading partner, it was a sign of his enthusiasm that he'd decided to leave his office and greet his new client on his arrival in the lobby. This was an extraordinary courtesy, and it was his expectation that any sane person, even this one, would acknowledge and appreciate it. This would give him what was most important in every situation: an edge.

Instead, when the elevator from the parking garage below opened, Field was the one taken by surprise. Will emerged not alone, but trailed by an imposing black man pushing a woman in a wheelchair.

"Ah, good" the attorney greeted the agent, "I'm not gonna have to pay for this, am I?" He held up his parking ticket.

"No, my assistant will validate that for you." He paused, waiting to be introduced to the others, but Will just stared up at him. "On behalf of the entire Talent Without Borders team, I bid you welcome."

"Do I give it to the assistant when we get up, or after?"

And this guy really thought he could beat Will Tripp in the game of keeping the other guy off balance?

"Anytime," said Field abjectly. He pressed the button for the elevator that led directly to his office, and stepped aside to let the others enter.

"We've only been here six months," he tried again, brightly, as he pushed 21. "So much space, I'm still finding my way around. And it's looking like we might have to take *another* floor."

Will nodded, but they rode the rest of the way in silence.

The elevator opened onto a vast waiting area. Behind the reception desk sat a young woman – face and upper chest-wise, at least, one of the most stunning Will had ever seen, and Field was pleased to note his interest. He had still not introduced his companions.

"Good to see you, Claire," he said, casually proprietary, as they moved past.

"The inner sanctum," he announced, as they followed him into a wide hallway lined with photos of agency clients, and watched with pride as they took them in: Brad Pitt, Emma Stone, Robin Williams, Selena Gomez, Sean Connery, Chris Pine, Mark Wahlberg, Zachary Quinto, Burt Reynolds, Denzel Washington, Alex Trabek...

"A lot of them are dead," said Will.

"We don't like to use that word, we prefer 'unavailable.'"

"Now, then," he said a few moments later, leading the way into his vast corner, and indicating the conference area, "please make yourselves comfortable."

Will climbed onto the couch, Arthur took the chair by the window, Marjorie stayed in her chair.

In seconds, the agent's assistant, Keith, appeared. "May I get you something to drink?"

"Anything you want," said Field, "we're a full service agency."

"You got something fizzy with mango?" By now this was Will's reflexive non-alcoholic beverage of choice; so much so, he was concerned he might be starting to lose his bearings.

"Manarango Frizz? Certainly."

"And you?" said Field, turning to Marjorie anxiously.

"They'll both have the same," said Will.

"Three Manarangos, got it!"

"Thank ze, Keith," said Field, as the assistant walked from the room, before turning to Will with a look somewhere between proud and apologetic. "Hir is nonbinary, I had to learn all that shit."

"I pity you!"

"And I'll take that pity and raise you disgust!" he said, grinning, but quickly added, "Only kidding."

"Are you?"

"Okay, then," he said, clapping his hands, "let's get to it!"

He paused, trying to decide whether to include the others, and how. Marjorie gazed at him with an eerie smile, and in the corner Arthur had begun playing with his phone. "I assume," he said, turning back to Will, "we can talk openly?"

"Of course."

"I've been giving this a lot of thought. And, just between us, I've already had a few conversations with producers and studio executives. Everyone fucking *loves* the idea!"

"What idea?"

"You! You're the idea, the concept, the project, the whole shebang!" He threw out his arms expansively. "We play this right, you'll *own* this fucking town!" He paused, but Will showed nothing. "And that's just the start!"

"Do I really look that selfish to you?" demanded Will with sudden severity. "That egotistical?"

"No, no, I didn't mean to suggest…"

"What about THEM?" demanded the dwarf, indicating his companions.

Marjorie was now looking the agent's way with inexpressible sadness; Arthur XXX seemed ready to kill him.

"No, no, of course, them, too. The whole crew. That's the point, you've achieved great things *together*. Not to put too fine a point on it, but the diversity angle is one of the big selling points."

Keith reappeared, and placed the drinks before them, while the visitors examined him with new interest.

"Thank ze, Keith," said Field, and waited a moment before continuing. "Look, the story of what you've done, all of you, is *epic*!"

"I thought you were interested in the sexy teachers cases."

"I *am*, that's part of it. They fucking *love* that – all that sex, and none of it *gratuitous*. Know what Linda Avakian called it? 'A goddamn wet dream!' Direct quote."

"Who?"

"But don't quote me on that. The head of production at Precision Pictures, that's all! One of the smartest people out here!"

"That's the studio that fired Michael Sawyer," said Will.

"Yeah, I know," he acknowledged, with a fleeting expression of regret, "She's extremely anxious to meet you."

"And I her!!"

"Excellente! I know you'll be impressed." He beamed, then looked sober again. "That was something a lot of us in this business had to learn, true, deep and abiding respect for women. Some of us now wake up every day and the first thing we feel is shame for how it used to be in this town."

Will nodded briskly. "Well, look forward to meeting her, got some questions."

"You won't be disappointed, I'll set it up." He dropped his voice. "Aside from everything else, she's got the best ass in the business."

It was not until they were in the elevator, heading down to the parking garage, that Will turned to Arthur. "Got it?"

Arthur held up his phone. "Every word."

For a dogged investigator like Danny Valenzuela, even in the internet age a good public library could be priceless, and Lafayette's on West Congress Street was state-of-the-art.

Yes, the woman at the second floor information desk assured him, they had the entire run of the city's newspaper, *The Daily Advertiser*. "We've it digitized, right from the beginning. 1865 right up to today."

"From just after the Civil War…"

She nodded. "Colonel William Bailey, the founder, he was on General Longstreet's staff." Her voice dropped. "Until just recently there was a statue of him out in Veterans Park."

"No more?"

The look she gave him let him know she didn't approve, and her voice dropped even lower. "No more."

The Advertiser had long covered not just Lafayette, but the region's six vast surrounding counties. They included the P.I.'s target area, the parishes of Iberia, Acadia and Vermilion.

Taking a seat at a carrel furnished with a computer pre-set to the library's data base, he accessed *The Daily Advertiser*'s file and typed in the name "Kevin Broussard."

He was surprised, and momentarily pleased, to find multiple references, filling a full screen and continuing to the next. But he quickly saw most were attached to wedding announcements, real estate transactions, or obituaries, and that some of these went back more than a century. *His* Kevin Broussard was, at most, 40 – his younger pal Guerin was 36 — so the listings he was seeking, if they could be found, probably would have occurred in the mid to late '90s, when he was in his teens. So the P.I. refined his search accordingly, to be safe, calling up the years 1993-2003.

Now there remained just a handful of references, and on closer examination, they referred to a mere two Kevin Broussards. One was the recently born, then the newly christened, child of a local pharmacist in St. Elizabethville; the other a decorated World War II vet in Lafayette who, his grieving daughter said, "brought sunshine into all our lives."

Reading this last, it once again struck Danny that very soon there'd be none of his cohort left and, the way things were going, they'd probably be little better remembered than William Baily.

Disappointed as he was, he wasn't close to giving up. A lot of people down here went by initials, so he next tried simply "K. Broussard," and there were indeed three of those. But two were women, the second a murder victim.

He moved on to the state's largest paper, New Orleans' *Times-Picayune*. It also had a fair number of Kevin and K. Broussards – the name seeming to be akin down here to Brown, if not quite Smith – although somewhat fewer than in the bayou region. And, again, no hits.

"Find what you're looking for?" asked the woman at the reference desk, brightly.

"Afraid not."

"If it's something historic, something like that, we do have books…"

"No, I'm pretty sure it would be of only local interest."

"Oh, I see. I'm so sorry."

But as he was walking toward the exit, she called. "Sir…"

He turned back.

"You might try SWL."

"SWL?"

"Southwestern Louisiana University, down by Vincennes. They keep all kinds of old newspapers there."

He'd been in the Louisiana Room on the third floor of SWL's Duprea Library less than three minutes before Danny knew he'd hit the mother lode. The laminated list of school's holdings in its newspaper archive included hundreds of periodicals, some actually predating the Louisiana Purchase, and among them were a dozen or so that had focused on Vermilion Parish, the area where Marc Guerin and his cohorts had come of age. The publications were all now defunct. But the last to go, *The Auvergne Vanguard*, had survived until 2008, when it was done in by the financial collapse.

None of the papers in this archive had been digitized, but some, including *The Vanguard*, were on microfilm, and within minutes, a student librarian was helping Valenzuela thread a reel labeled '*Auverge Vanguard*, 1992-1993,' into the old fashioned viewing machine.

As he slowly turned the crank, scanning the weekly's pages on the screen, as expected he mainly found news of exceedingly local interest — charity lunches, births and deaths, minor car accidents. Yet in every issue, there appeared on page two a Police Blotter, and he read each of these more carefully. Overwhelmingly, they were given over to DWI's, shoplifters and bar fights. One such altercation between a tourist from Texas and the bouncer at a local bar had resulted in a hospital stay for one and a night in the lockup for the other.

As he grew familiar with the sameness of the issues, he moved faster, stopping now and then to learn a bit more of a feud between local politicians or examine the photos of that year's King Gabriel and Queen Evangeline and their respective courts in that year's Mardi Gras festivities.

He spent an hour and a half at the machine with this single reel, but by the time he was on to the next, 1994-1995, he was moving quickly enough to get through it in under and hour; and he was done with the one that followed, 1996-1997, even faster.

He'd arrived at 10:30, and it was now past 2:00, and after having been so hopeful, he was starting to feel the first stirrings of discouragement. He'd noticed there was a Popeye's just outside the campus, and thought of taking a break, but brushed the idea aside, and kept going. It had taken him more than an hour to drive here, and the library closed at five; he could just about get through the rest.

He requested the next tape, 1998-1999, and was past the midpoint, when his cranking hand stopped cold.

A banner headline on page one of the August 19, 1999 issue read: LOCAL YOUTHS CHARGED IN HIJACK.

Directly beneath, in grainy black and white on the screen, appeared a photo of three teens. In the caption, they were identified as Claude Leroy, John K. Broussard, Jr., and Robert Peedee, Jr. They were in handcuffs, each accompanied by a uniformed officer, and two of them were looking down at the ground in sullen shame. But the one in the middle, Kevin, stares coolly back at the camera.

The details were in the accompanying story. According to police, the accused had intercepted a truck delivering stereo equipment on a little travelled Highway 10A between Varennes and St. Jacques, first blocking the road with their own vehicle, a 1993 Chevrolet Caprice. After pistol whipping the driver, 52, a father of six, and warning him to keep quiet, they'd left him hogtied in his truck. He had been rescued by a passing motorist, who reported the crime to police from a roadside booth, before proceeding to a hospital, where the driver was reported to be in stable condition. The boys were arrested in Julien two hours later.

Peedee was a big kid, more fat than muscle, already on his way to full-blown obese, given the crap they stuffed themselves with down here. He had to be the one called Tiny.

And since Kevin was Bayou, the P.I. figured the wiry, furtive-looking Leroy to be Yoda.

But there was one other detail of even greater interest to the investigator than the rest. "According to Officer Jenkins, there was in addition a fourth youth involved. However, he is underage for charges as an adult, and at this writing a decision on his status is pending."

For Will, here was more proof Noah Field couldn't be trusted! Linda Avakian's ass was certainly passable, but no way was it one of the *best* in town! This was not up for debate; as Precision Pictures' head of production gave her visitors a tour of the studio lot, he'd dropped back a few paces so had a perfect view. He saw better every day through his car window right here in L.A., artful products of private trainers and endless workout hours. Hell, only minutes before he'd seen a pair of better ones on this very lot, side by side, on actresses done up as EMT's.

Then, again, in fairness, everyone exaggerated out here. The place was Fantasyland! Far more likely, in this case, is that hers was simply among the best asses to kiss.

"You know," she was saying, as she paused to let the lawyer catch up, "originally this was Harold Lloyd's studio. Do you know his work?"

The question seemed to be directed at Marjorie, in her chair, the only other woman in the group, but as instructed, she remained silent, and Field jumped in. "One of the great silent clowns! A genius of the first rank!"

The studio honcho caught the dwarf lawyer shoot his new agent a look of loathing and contempt.

"Have you seen any Lloyd pictures, Mr. Tripp?"

"I have. Not funny."

Caught short, she laughed. "You know, I happen to agree with you," She put a finger to her lips. "But quiet."

"Me too!" exclaimed Field, "That's what I really think." He beamed at the studio executive. "See what I mean about this guy, Linda?"

Linda Avakian was 42, and already it was apparent to the dwarf lawyer why she had gotten so far, so fast. She was smart, confident and approachable, with a warm, easy laugh; and in thousand dollar slacks, with that perfectly okay ass, kind've sexy. But it was also hard to miss the strength of the steel beneath the charm.

Having graduated from Stanford with a degree in film studies, she'd started in the business producing small, independent features before moving into the executive ranks. Her career had been made by having fought for a project no one else believed in, but *Fast, Faster, Fastest* earned over $500 million worldwide, and turned an unknown Marc Guerin into an international sensation.

A couple of years into her second marriage to a green energy billionaire, she of course still went by her original name, which Will had to remind himself was *not* Kasabian, that was a Manson girl.

Not that it was likely to come up, no one used last names out here.

"I love movie history" she said now, "actually, all history, don't you, Will?"

"Yes, I do, Linda. And, please, Mr. Tripp."

"I personally love that our industry is such a *fantastic* teaching tool," Fields hastily picked up the thread. "My own kids, everything they know about history is from the movies."

"Which ones?" asked Will, dubiously.

"Yes, which ones?" said Linda, pleased she and the dwarf lawyer were on common ground. "That's the important question, isn't it? Because, as we know, too many of the films we've made have presented a tragically distorted view of America's past. Isn't that so, Wi...Mr. Tripp?"

"Absolutely, Linda."

"Even many so-called classics, like *The Searchers,*" said Linda, with sudden passion. "Its depiction of native peoples...really, it's almost criminally inaccurate."

"That's so true," agreed Will. The picture, about John Wayne's endless search for the niece captured in childhood and raised by redskins, was one of his all-time favorites. "The Comanches were so much more bloodthirsty than they showed. In reality, they used to torture their enemies by staking them spread eagle naked over beds of red ants..."

"Anyway," cut in Field, "I'm sure we can agree that..."

"...and they'd bury captives up to the neck with their eyelids cut off so they'd go blind from the sun before starving to death."

There was a long moment of silence.

"What did I tell you," said Field, uneasily, "isn't he *fantastic?*"

"I was fully prepared for Mr. Tripp," she replied, with a suddenly cool smile. "I looked at the material you sent over personally." She paused. "Actually, I'm a bit confused. Aren't you also representing Michael Sawyer in his absurd suit?"

Will nodded. "I am."

"But that's not why we're here," interjected Field. "He's got a fantastic, unique story to tell…"

"Well, I'll save you a lot of trouble," she said, ignoring this. "I'm sorry Michael feels slighted, but there is nothing to discuss. We were never going to make *New Orleans*, let alone hire him in a principal role."

"He signed a contract."

"But Marc Guerin didn't, and he's the only reason we'd ever even consider moving ahead with such a film."

"I understood Guerin had committed."

"Marc commits to everything, he's notoriously fickle — it's the prerogative of genius."

Field caught Will's eye and gave a helpless shrug, mouthing the words "It's true."

"You should know it has come to our attention that Sawyer only procured a copy of this script in the first place, which was studio property, through theft. And we *will* prosecute."

In a flash, the attorney knew where she'd come by this information: Evan! The little creep was obviously hoping to slither upward from Bar Mitzvahs to the big time!

Will tried to look like he'd been hit by the verbal equivalent of a Mack truck, even as inwardly he smiled at the thought of what they didn't yet know: their boy, Guerin, was the real deal, a *bona fide* armed robber.

"And you of course know Sawyer's contract had a morality clause," she pressed her advantage.

"And so...?" he ventured uncertainly.

"Just for your information, because we certainly have no interest in this being made public, the flag flying and the hate speech are just the tip of the iceberg. Did you know Michael Sawyer drives a car with a gasoline engine, and uses oil to heat his home? Are you aware that when living in Missouri, before moving to this state, he was registered as a Republican?" She leaned forward for the clincher. "Do you know, Mr. Tripp, that Michael Sawyer once owned a *rifle?*"

Looking crushed, Will said nothing, as she sat back in her chair.

"This is new information," he replied finally,

"Well, I just thought you should know, because there should be no secrets between us. If he pursues this, he's dead in this town."

"I'll speak to my client."

She smiled. "But on to more pleasant things – *The Will Tripp Story.*"

"Aka *Attorney for the Damned,*" said Field, with undimmed enthusiasm.

"We think it's a *very* intriguing notion." She paused. "It hits a lot of the right chords. I love the politically incorrect angle – people just hate PC, the time couldn't be better."

"Yes!"

"Of course, we have to be careful, we wouldn't want to seem to be on the wrong side..." She considered, with furrowed brow. "That'll be the trick, won't it? For instance, how do we show, between the lines, that it was the patriarchy that distorted the schoolteacher's values? Should we make her black, to raise systemic racism, or make one of the boys gay? Or would that be seen as tokenism?"

"I see what you mean," managed Will thoughtfully, masking his revulsion. If humanity itself depended on it, no way he'd ever allow this horror show on the air.

"Great problems to have!" said Field, adding with a hand sweep that took in the pair of silent associates, "and what a supporting cast!"

Arthur, Will was pleased to note, casually held his phone at an angle suggesting he might be getting not just audio, but video.

"I'll tell you something," mused Avakian. "I think Marc will absolutely *love* it."

"Wow!" said Field.

"I think with a little nudge, we could get him to commit."

"'Commit' in what way?" asked Will, recalling what they'd been saying barely five minutes before,

"To play you!"

"Really?" To the extent he'd allowed himself to consider it, Will had naturally assumed they'd get one of the current performing dwarves, Peter Dinklage or the English guy, Warwick Davis, who, like Will, stood a healthy three foot six.

"It's the movies, *that's* how!" said Avakian, smiling at the newcomer's apparent skepticism. "Think Daniel Day-Lewis really had that disease where he could only use his left foot?"

"Ah," Will nodded, even as he recognized the absurdity of the comparison.

"I could talk to Bernie Richards," suggested Field.

"Who's that?"

"Marc's manager. Crazy fuck, but a great guy. A visionary."

"Or better yet," suggested Avakian, "why not have Bernie get together with Mr. Tripp."

"Please," he allowed graciously, "Will." He smiled. "I'd love that — I'm known to be pretty persuasive."

He didn't know which was more appalling, that they thought he could be bought so cheaply, or that even for an instant, however fleetingly, they might have been right.

"Fan-fucking-tastic," exulted Field, "I'll set it up!"

Moments later, as they got up to leave, with handshakes all around, the studio exec at last addressed Will's associates.

"Do you two speak?"

"Yes," said Arthur, glaring.

"Of ccccccccccourse."

"She has a little speech impediment," explained Will. "As well as crippled."

"They have real law degrees?"

"They do. Passed the bar, and everything."

The executive looked from one to the other, beaming. "How'd you like to be Vice President for Legal Affairs here at Precision Pictures?"

"What about Larry Jaffe?" wondered Field, the incumbent being another of his close friends.

"Larry's a team player, he'll understand..." She looked again at her would-be hires, and nodded dismissively at Will. "We'll double whatever he's paying."

Taken by surprise, the dwarf attorney was already sensing opportunity. "Which one are you asking?" he inquired evenly.

"Either. Or both!" Her eyes were alive at the prospect. If she could make it happen, she'd be the envy of every studio head in town.

"Well, the three of us will have to discuss it," said Will. "I really don't know if I could function without them."

Well as the meeting had gone, this may have been the topper! Suddenly, out of the blue, he found himself with an asset that, in a town where decency was always for sale, was valuable beyond calculation: something everyone wanted.

This time, sitting at the same carrel in the Lafayette Public Library, Danny Valenzuela knew exactly what he was looking for. While there had been no follow up in the local weekly on the arrest of the three boys, he expected to find at least passing reference to the disposition of the case in *The Daily Advertiser.*

Accessing its database, he typed in the name: John K. Broussard, Jr.

Disappointed, he waited a moment, then tried the name without the "K; then without the "Jr."

Still nothing. It was looking like a dead end.

So when he tried "Claude Leroy," he was actually surprised when three listings appeared on the screen. The first was a brief item published, along with several others, on May 4, 2008, under the general heading Crime Report. "A Clarence man, identified as Claude Leroy, 26, was charged with larceny, after an employee of Lovett Jewelers on Second Street discovered the man attempting to exit the establishment with three Xerix brand watches, and a gold bracelet, valued in total at $1,500. Leroy, who has a prior felony conviction for armed robbery of a delivery truck, was held at Lafayette Parish, prior to being released on his own recognizance, pending an appearance Monday before Judge Piccarello in City Court."

The P.I. glanced down at the grainy photo he'd had copied previously. Leroy/Yoda was 17 then, and obviously terrified and desperate, and who could guess at all that must have gone wrong.

The next item appeared five years later, on August 18, 2013, under the headline: MAN VIOLATES ORDER, TERRORIZES WIFE. "A St. Elizabeth man, 31, is in custody today, after violating a court order taken by his estranged wife, Renee Leroy, 37, and forcibly entering her residence on South Champaign Blvd. Responding to a frantic call from the woman saying the man was brandishing a knife and menacing her with bodily injury, police said on their arrival he failed to respond to their orders to desist and had to be tased. A kitchen knife was recovered at the scene. Leroy subsequently tested positive for the hallucinogen PCP."

The final item was dated March 14, 2017: TRAFFIC STOP LEADS TO COCAINE BUST. "A local man is facing felony drug charges, after police found one and a half kilograms (3.30 pounds) of cocaine in his vehicle following a routine traffic stop. Claude Leroy of St. Elizabethville, 35, was seen by police to be seen driving erratically, as well as not wearing a seat belt, when he was pulled over on the 400 block of Southfield. A spokesman for the Lafayette Parish Sheriff's Office later said the drugs, which have an estimated value in excess of $50,000, were clearly visible on the back floor of the vehicle. The arrested man is expected to be charged with possession with intent to distribute, as well as carrying a weapon in the presence of a controlled substance."

This was great stuff, and as he typed in Robert Peedee, Jr. Valenzuela was hoping for still more. Sure enough, there was a listing – just one, but it stopped the P.I. cold: LOCAL MAN, 36, FOUND DEAD OUTSIDE BAR, read the November 4, 2015 headline. "A 36-year-old Abbeville man, identified as Robert Peedee, Jr., was discovered deceased this morning outside the Crawford Brasserie, a bar and restaurant in Abbeville. 'He was a little unsteady on his feet, and he said he was going outside to get some air,' said Del Crawford, the bar's owner. 'When he didn't come back, we thought he'd gone home.' However, Peedee, described as an unemployed construction worker, was discovered this morning in an alley a mere 20 feet from the entrance. He was pronounced dead at the scene of an apparent heart attack. 'If we'd known he was out there, maybe we could've done something.' said Crawford, adding that Peedee was a regular customer, and 'a great guy.' At this writing there is no report of survivors or funeral arrangements."

Synergistics, Bernie Richards' company, maintained a small office in Beverly Hills, but Guerin's manager mainly worked out of his home in Los Feliz, and this is where he proposed that he and the dwarf lawyer meet.

On his own, Will decided to bring along Arthur XXX Perkins. In this case it was not for the usual reason — to throw the other guy off his game — but to help sell Marc Guerin's manager on *Attorney for the Damned*; and, more, arrange a face-to-face between the dwarf lawyer and the star himself. In his dual role as Will's associate and model for a leading character in the proposed series, Arthur had been reminded to keep the scowling to a minimum. The object was to ingratiate, not intimidate.

But when Richards threw open the door to the secluded bungalow, it was the visitors who were taken by surprise. Richards was tiny, a mere foot and a half taller than Will, and dressed, elf-like, entirely in red – red shirt, red pants, candy cane striped socks, Adidas running shoes. And at his side, towering over him, was the largest Great Dane they'd ever seen, 200 pounds of muscle panting menacingly.

"Welcome to our abode," said Richards cheerfully, in a high-tone English accent. "I'm Bernie, and this is Master Lord Shiva."

"Oh," mumbled Will, "after the Hindu god."

"Exactly! The destroyer *and* the restorer," he said, meaningfully. "Do come in."

The odor hit them as soon as they walked through the door, so overpowering it made the dwarf's head swim. Dog shit! There were piles of it, mounds, here and there on the tile floors in every direction.

Noting Arthur starting to gag, Richards nodded sympathetically. "I do understand," he said. "Yet who are we to impose our values on our fellow beings? Who's to say this place is any more mine than Lord Shiva's?"

"Who, indeed?" Will gasped in agreement.

"You paid for it," observed Arthur.

"Yes, in *this* world I did," he answered mysteriously, ushering them past a large mound into the living room "But not in *every* world…"

Trying not to be obvious, they chose their chairs carefully….

"A beverage?" said Richards. "I understand you're Manarango men."

"You're too kind," said Will, with a gesture of his tiny hand, impressed that he'd obviously done his research, "but not just now."

"Mr. Perkins? Or do you prefer XXX?"

"Nothing right now," said Arthur; then, following his boss's lead, "but you're too kind."

Their host climbed into a chair facing them both, as the dog took up his post alongside. "Now, then, about this most thrilling project of yours..."

"We think so."

"Oh, yes, unquestionably." He paused. "Our job, Master Lord Shiva's and mine, is of course to assess whether the material is appropriate for Marc Guerin."

"Of course."

"Whether it serves his larger purposes, not simply in terms of career, but as part of his *human* mission in this realm."

For real, Will thought he might puke. "We understand."

"That is the essence of the third eye, which speaks to perception, far-sightedness, even, if you will, clairvoyance. It is what enabled me more than ten years ago to so clearly perceive in Marc Guerin what others of far greater experience had missed, that this was a young man blessed with a gift granted to perhaps one in a 100 million."

"Right," managed Will, "he's a good actor."

"It's only now the town is beginning to acknowledge his astonishing range," rhapsodized the other, "and understand there is nothing he cannot do!"

"So...has Marc seen the material?"

"And his instincts are flawless," he ignored the question. "While not necessarily book smart, no one is more in touch with his chakras. I facilitate, but he is spiritually far more advanced, and I must do my best to just try and keep pace."

"Has he seen the material?" Will asked again.

"He has, and he loves it!"

"Wonderful!"

"He believes the part will stretch him as both an actor and a living being in quite meaningful ways."

"Great! Really eager to meet him!"

"And he you! I shall see to it."

"Wonderful!"

Richards began climbing down from his chair, which Will took to mean he should do likewise, and the manager approached, hand extended.

"You can imagine why I was so taken with your story."

"Of course" he said, shaking the other's hand. "I'm really taken by your clothes."

"As long as we're doing business, have you signed yet with Noah Field?"

Will was actually a bit disappointed; he'd thought the spiritual bullshit, beyond being useful career-wise, might be for real. Not, of course, that out here that was necessarily a contradiction. "Not yet," he replied, "we've got a handshake deal."

"Don't, not before checking with me."

"You got it."

Richards nodded toward Arthur, edging hopefully toward the front door, and dropped his voice. "What about Arthur?"

"What about him?"

"How much?"

"Sorry, he's not for sale."

Richards looked stunned, and a little hurt, and Will suddenly realized it might queer the deal.

"I just need him too much," he said, loud enough for Arthur to hear. "Arthur's very special, he went to Harvard."

"*Really?*" said the other, his interest even more intense.

"Affirmative action," called Arthur dismissively, sensing where this was going.

"Even so." His boss shot him a look, he was expected to take one for the team; they'd discussed the possibility earlier. "He's absolutely brilliant, has his finger firmly on the nation's pulse! Show him Arthur."

Arthur gave a reluctant sigh. "Institutional racism," he intoned. "Social justice. Diversity."

"More, flash that vocabulary."

Arthur paused, considering. "Antidisestablishmentarianism."

"See that, the longest word in the whole damn dictionary!"

"I've got to have him!"

Will sighed in surrender. "Well, I guess that's that, I can't stand in the way of Arthur's career."

Ten minutes later, walking back toward their waiting limo, Arthur laid out the deal he'd negotiated, and Will was dumbstruck. It was better than anything he could have come up with himself.

Arthur was to be named president and CEO of Third Eye Synergistics, with a whopping increase over his current salary and no defined duties, other than to be pictured in ads and brochures; while Richards, assuming the lesser title of executive vice president, would continue to do all the work.

Will studied his protégé – for at last that's what he truly was – with new eyes. "Anything else?"

"You kidding, boss? – the most important thing. I won't be working here, but out of the Beverly Hills place."

"What the papers didn't say," laughed Del Crawford, from behind the bar, "is when they found Tiny, he had his pecker in his hand." He laughed again, "Poor sonovabitch was out there takin' a piss."

"Del's just gildin' the lily," chuckled the guy in the Saints cap on the stool beside Danny, "his fly was open, is all."

"Uh uh, don' tell me, I seen it, the media jus' didn't think that little detail was, what do they call it, *family* friendly."

The several other guys listening in laughed along with the owner.

"Well, guess no need for the poor bastard to suffer that final indignity," offered one.

"That was Tiny, all right," said another, "a class act 'til the end."

Del turned back to Danny with a slight shrug. "Really, not much more to tell. Sad but familiar tale, man died like he lived…"

It was a little past eight on a Wednesday night, the P.I. had rightly guessed the place wouldn't be crowded, and that those present would likely be longtime regulars.

"So he came here a lot…"

"Tiny?" He laughed. "Oh, yeah."

"Tragic loss," said someone else. "He was Del's best customer."

Crawford nodded. "There was times he'd be waitin' when I opened, and then he'd still be here when I closed. One of those."

"A lush, straight-up," said the guy in the Saints cap.

"Jus' a sad case. There were times he could be the life of the party, laughin' and jokin', but even then you might catch him, hunched over his drink, and he'd be 300 pounds've sadness."

Danny sipped his beer – it was the house special, from a new craft brewery in nearby Mandeville. "The article said he was in construction?"

"Jus' now and then," said Crawford." He paused. "Wasn't easy, he had a record…"

"Right," said Danny. He paused. "What was that all about, what'd he do?"

"Him an' a couple've of his boys knocked off a truck," someone said.

"Prison system wrecked him," interjected Crawford, with unexpected vehemence. "He was a one man case for prison reform!"

"Uh oh, Del, don't get started."

"Jus' sayin'," shot back the bar owner. "He was just a stupid little kid when they put him in…"

"Not so little…"

"And also guilty as charged," pointed out the guy in the cap.

"Well, two years later, he comes out, an' he jus' a big sack've messed up.'"

Danny himself was a lock-em-up, throw-away-the-key kind've guy, *but* he was impressed; Crawford was a true barroom bard.

"Nobody didn't like Tiny," added the guy in the cap after a moment. "He was…"

"His heart was big as his ass," agreed Del.

There was a long, reflective pause. Then one of the men cracked. "That was a moment of silence for the fat fuck."

Danny laughed with the others, then returned to where he'd started. "So he talk much about his friend Marc?"

"You kidding? Couldn't get him to shut up."

Danny nodded. "Must've been a huge deal for a guy like that, must've made him feel important."

"We're all proud of Marc 'round here," one of the others spoke for the first time. He had a heavy Acadian accent, which made it sound a like a warning.

"Sure. Not the first time I've heard that."

"Proudest moment of Tiny's life was when Marc came back to be the king of the Mardi Gras parade in Lafayette. Ol' Tiny got to ride up on the float right beside him. *Never* stopped talking about that."

"Sure, must've been pretty special."

"Fact is," said Crawford, "Tiny first started goin' on about Marc before anyone even knew who he was. He'd go on an' on about his friend out in Hollywood, and we figured it was jus' more of Tiny's hooey. Hollywood? Might as well've been talkin' about Mars. Then that first big movie of his came out…"

"*Fast, Faster, Fastest…*" said the P.I.

"…and, good Christ, it was true! An' suddenly it's like *Tiny's* a star, with people wantin' to get their picture took with him, and then people like you start comin' from places like New York, wantin' to talk to him…"

"Right, sure…" Danny had perused some of those early, over-the-top Guerin profiles in places like *People* and *Entertainment Weekly.*

"…An', course, nobody was more ready to talk than ol' Tiny. But right, then, jus' when he was gettin' to enjoy it…" Crawford smiled wistfully. "Tiny never did have any kind've luck but bad."

"Well, I guess the lesson is, go to Del's, use the men's room…"

"Right, it's *dangerous* out there," laughed one of the others, "no tellin' what might happen."

There was something in the way he said it that gave the P.I. pause. "Well," he observed carefully. "Guy that big" – he snapped his fingers – "sometimes the heart just goes. Wouldn't've mattered where he was."

This was met with silence.

"Maybe," allowed Crawford, finally. He looked at his friends, a couple smiled. "*Probably.*"

Am I missing something?"

"You feel like tellin' it, Del…?" asked the guy in the cap.

Crawford studied Danny a moment. "Oh, hell, guess it don't matter now." He paused. "See, the thing is, him bein' out there was the whole thing."

"What do you mean?"

He paused. "Well, Tiny went out there to do his business, all right, but it wasn't no heart attack that got him."

Valenzuela nodded, showing nothing. "What was it?"

"He was pretty far gone that night, even for him, so after we did feel bad, like we failed him…"

"Right…"

"It had been rainin' pretty hard that day." He hesitated. "When we found him, he was face down in a puddle. Nothin' to do then but drag him out."

Danny nodded. "I see. That's something, all right."

"Wouldn't've been great publicity, either. Sumbitch comes in for liquid refreshment, and ends up drowning hisself in four inches of water."

"Truly pathetic," said Will, on hearing the story that evening. "Talk about a loser!"

Valenzuela smiled, shaking his head. "And I defend you when people say you're a heartless little prick!"

"Waah, waah, waah." Will did his baby imitation, balled fists rubbing his eyes, then switched to making like he was playing a violin.

"I feel bad for the guy, sue me."

"So what's your read, an accident or...?"

"Like the man said, *probably*." Danny paused. "That's definitely what those guys think – they were there, and they're straight shooters..."

"On the other hand..."

"Right, Tiny was a loudmouth, desperate for attention..."

"And there's the timing. Just when the media assholes were starting to show up, poking into Guerin's past."

The P.I. couldn't help but chuckle. "We really are a pair of *cabrones paranoicos*, aren't we?"

"*Paranoid?*" said the dwarf attorney. "Goddamn right, I take that as a compliment."

The P.I. considered. "You know, if it was just this one thing, Tiny conveniently dying..."

Will waited a moment for him to continue. "But...?"

"Well, just to be sure, I checked out the files at the Bureau of Prisons. Sure enough, there's no record that Guerin was involved with that armed robbery..."

This was the opposite of a bombshell. "Right, he was a juvenile – tell me something I don't know."

"How's this? — there's no record for Kevin Broussard, either."

"Nothing?"

"No criminal record of any kind." He paused. "Whatever there was has been expunged."

"You're kidding me."

"Clean as a whistle. Same way I couldn't find his name in *The Daily Advertiser* file."

"Whoa!" exclaimed Will. "That doesn't happen — not with a Class A felony."

"Takes a ton of pull. And mucho, *mucho* dinero."

"Any idea who handled the case?"

"I'm on it. From what I'm told so far, had to have been one of the big connected law firms in Baton Rouge, and a very open-minded judge with pockets wide open as the great outdoors."

The dwarf lawyer whistled his amazement. This was interesting indeed!

"What about the third guy, Leroy...?"

"Yoda?" said Valenzuela, who'd come to think of them all by their alternate names. "Looks like he also got kid glove treatment for a while. The first felony, the jewelry store theft, he got off with a week of community service..."

"Well, basically that was a glorified shoplift."

"Still, the guy was a fuck-up and already probably using. No question he was when he went after the ex-wife with a knife. He was obviously high as a kite on angel dust." He paused. "Walked on that also."

"Nothing?"

"Nothing. Charges dismissed."

"Jesus!"

"But on the last one..."

"...the cocaine bust..."

"Caught red handed, with intent to sell," said the P.I. "And this time got treated like any other three-time loser." He snorted. "Asshole helping him ran out of patience."

"Friendship has its limits..."

There was no wondering who they were talking about.

"So the dumbass is in prison now?"

"You got it. Mandatory 10 to 15. And down here, that's *hard* time."

"Will he see you...?"

Valenzuela hesitated. "That's the question – Yoda's never been a big talker, not like Tiny." He paused. "I wrote him this morning, appealed to his vanity. We'll see."

"If he's got a brain in his head, he'll tell you to go screw yourself."

"True."

"The good news is we're talking about a guy who gets busted for not putting on his seatbelt."

"The even better news is he just lost his appeal, he's not getting out of that hellhole anytime soon."

"Guessing he didn't have much of a case."

"Or much of a lawyer — had some Legal Aid bum, who probably gave his case ten minutes between sex offenders."

"So he's pissed…"

"Let's hope he's been sitting there stewing about it — about Bayou…and his long lost friend out in Hollywood…"

The tiny town of Varennes was little different from most others in Iberville Parish, a handful of small stores and a collection of ramshackle homes, some well-kept but mostly not.

Danny had no idea if it would help, but it was four days since he'd sent his letter to Yoda, and it probably wouldn't hurt.

Pulling up to the lone pump beside a general store, he got out, just as an old Vietnamese woman emerged from the store.

"Full?" she asked, revealing a heavy accent in a single syllable.

"Please."

He waited until she was done before showing her the slip of paper with the address that, misdirected by Google, he'd spent the previous twenty minutes driving in circles looking for: 14 Constellation Drive.

"There," she said, nodding vaguely in the direction from which he'd come. "Road back there."

"Is it far?"

"No far, right near." She pointed, "Two minute."

He'd missed the road both because it was unmarked and because it was scarcely identifiable as a road at all – more like a path, barely wide enough for a car. It led to a trailer park, meandering between rows of motor homes mounted on cinderblocks.

Each such home was numbered, lending the place an air of at least semi-permanence. He found number 14 toward the back. The unit looked older than most of the others, probably dating to the '80s. White with silver trim and in good repair, it was set back from the road ten yards or so, creating a small front yard, and bricks had been placed on the ground, making a walkway. On either side were neatly tended flowerbeds.

The P.I. parked and headed up the walkway.

At his ring, there came a raspy voice from somewhere nearby. "Come on 'round."

He looked for the speaker.

"'Round back."

Walking around the trailer, there were more flowers, and a plastic rocking horse and children's toys scattered on the patch of lawn. The man who'd called sat in a dilapidated wicker chair, in old jeans and a blue windbreaker, and he was smoking a cigarette. The P.I. put him in his early sixties.

"How you doin'?" the man greeted him, with encouraging bonhomie, "Hope you ain't here to sell me nothin'."

Danny smiled. "Nothing like that. I'm looking for Ronald Leroy."

He looked surprised, but remained friendly. "You found 'im."

"Glad to hear it." Extending his hand, he approached the older man. "I'm Rich Hernandez, I'm a reporter. Doing a story on Marc Guerin."

Leroy shook his hand, but his voice went flat. "Yeah, well, sorry, we don't talk to reporters."

"It's just, I know he and your son were good buddies, really close."

"I know what it's about. But sorry."

Danny stood there a moment; it struck him the guy really did seem sorry.

"You been living here long?" he asked.

"Almost 35 years."

"What kind've work you do?"

"I know what you're doin', mister." Leroy smiled, but figured there was no harm. "You seen Dawes Rentals when you came through town – sugar cane and harvestin' equipment? I was there 28 years."

"So you raised your family here?"

"It's bigger n' it looks – we got two bedrooms. Our other boy, he lives right down the way – number seven." He nodded at the rocking horse. "We keep this kids' stuff here for my little granddaughter."

"I see. That's really nice."

"You got kids?" he asked.

Danny nodded. "A boy, 13. But his mother and me don't get along so well. We're divorced."

"Sorry to hear it. Terrible thing, divorce. Terrible for kids."

Amazing, thought Danny, that this guy raised a career criminal. "Please, sir," he said, "I've come a long way. I've just got a couple of questions."

The other took a long draw on his cigarette, shook his head. "Can't help you…"

"I just think your son's getting a raw deal."

That seemed to catch his interest.

"Seems like Marc stood by him for a while, but then walked away. I'm just trying to figure out what happened."

"Goddamn drugs, that's what happened," he said, less angry than hopeless.

"It must've been hard on you and your wife, that first time he got sent off to jail. He was only – what? – 17?"

"Sixteen, the first time."

"Seems that's all that saved Marc, being three years younger. Otherwise he'd've been sent away with the others."

"Prob'ly so."

In the momentary silence, there was the shared understanding of the meaning of a record – and, more precisely, of *not* having one – for someone looking to get ahead in the world.

"Listen, I'm not out to get Marc, I admire him like everyone else. But I think it's an important story. About friendship and how it can change over time, and how much it can hurt to lose it. I just want to tell the truth. And I'm pretty sure telling it can only help Claude."

"It's jus' he always tol' us not to have nothin' to do with you people."

Valenzuela nodded in understanding. "He was always unselfish, I get that. But now he's the one who needs help."

When the other didn't reply, he asked: "Just curious, back then, when they were young, would you say all four were equally close?"

"Oh, good gosh, mister, what a question!" he exclaimed. "How would I ever know a thing like that – they was *kids*!"

"I only ask cause these days he still seems so tight with Bayou…"

"Who's that?!"

Danny wheeled to see a heavyset woman in a black nylon waitress uniform beside the trailer.

"Oh, Grace," said the older, seeming to shrink to half the size in his chair, "this here is Mr…"

"Danny Hernandez, I'm from New York."

"…I was jus' tellin' him a little about our Claude…"

Her face went red so fast, it was like someone slapped her. "Goddamn it, Ronald, you *know* not to do that! Ain't he made that clear enough?"

"He jus' came by, Grace…"

"You, get out!" she said, turning on the P.I. "Whatever this fool told you, don' listen, it's crap."

"I understand," said Valenzuela, starting back around the building toward his car.

"You better! It's all — whatever they call it, off the damn record!"

The long-awaited meeting with Marc Guerin was set for 5:30, at the offices of Guerin's company, Zydeco Productions. Heading there in the limo, Marjorie at his side, Will again reviewed his file on the star. Not that there was much point, since the file consisted almost entirely of biographical stuff pulled from mainstream publications and gossip sheets; all the usual stuff, a good deal of it the product of P.R. departments. The only piece that deviated from the standard narrative — or, actually, augmented it in an interesting way — was the one from the student newspaper.

The truth is, even now the dwarf lawyer had no real sense of who his prey, Guerin, really was: how he behaved in private; what he thought and how he expressed it; how he'd gone from good ol' boy to Hollywood's most bare knuckled enforcer of the party line; whether he had even passing remorse about the part he played in the destruction of deviant thinkers like Michael Sawyer.

But that was okay. Chief among Will Tripp's many talents was his skill at improvisation. No one was better on his feet, or more readily able to ingratiate himself with others; and, before very long, induce them to reveal their weaknesses and vulnerabilities. Moreover, in this case, he'd have at the ready, if necessary, the information Danny had unearthed about his erstwhile pals back home.

They arrived at the sprawling Precision Pictures lot, where Zydeco was based, at 20 past, and met by the star's middle-aged English assistant, who icily introduced herself as Glynis.

"Sorry," she said, not sorry at all, "just now Marc is otherwise engaged."

"How long do you think he'll be?"

"You may wait here," she said, indicating the reception area.

"How long will he be?"

She all but rolled her eyes. "I don't know, he's watching the dailies, he cannot be interrupted."

"I see." Will suppressed his fury, considered how to proceed. "Please inform him," he said, with a British accent, "that I make a policy of not dealing with rude motherfuckers."

He turned back toward the elevator and Marjorie followed in her chair.

"No, please!" she cried in panic. "Wait!"

"And please inform him that I include you in that characterization."

"Bbbbbbbbitch!" murmured Marjorie, in support.

"You're right, I'm so very sorry," pleaded Glynis. "Please, please, *please* give me half a moment, I'm sure something can be done."

She rushed into an adjacent room, and they could hear her speaking desperately on the phone.

"Marc would *love* to have you join him," she beamed, coming back. "He believes your input will be invaluable."

"Just don't let it happen again!" allowed Will graciously.

As they headed toward the screening room, Glynis informed them they would be seeing brief bits of the star's current film-in-progress, entitled *Permanent Record*.

"High school picture?" speculated the dwarf attorney, lately having been immersed in the subject.

"Oh, no." She smiled and made a conscious effort not to sound condescending. "It's a metaphor, actually, it has to do with the terrible baggage people of color are made to carry in this country from birth until their dying day. This, you see, is their permanent record – it is always there, invisible yet inescapable."

"You're saying it's *not* about high school?" Will came back, disappointed. "Nothing about dating or proms, anything like that?"

"No, I'm afraid not." She hesitated. "It is the story of a decorated cop, he is the chief of the department in Houston, and through a series of events he comes to understand the depth of his own racism. This comes as a revelation, because he's always considered himself a good person."

"What events?" inquired Will earnestly, as if he too was given to such soul searching.

"Well, in the first act we learn that earlier he's beaten someone he'd arrested nearly to death, under the mistaken impression he was a person of color – and when he learns otherwise, in his torment and remorse, he decides to do whatever it takes to have *everyone* he's ever arrested, no matter their ethnicity, released from jail."

"I like it!" exulted Will. "It's what I always look for in jurors!"

"Yes, and one of these guys he gets out," she continued, "essentially becomes his conscience. First he makes him his spokesman, then his deputy, and finally he arranges to have himself replaced by this fellow as chief!"

"What was this guy convicted of?" asked Will.

"Armed robbery and kidnapping."

"Did he do it?"

"Immaterial," she smiled knowingly. "Doesn't matter. After all, that is precisely the question we in the audience are meant to ponder: What is 'guilt'" – she made quote marks with her fingers – "And the answer is, there's no such thing, it's merely a social construct."

"Ahhh…"

They'd taken an elevator down several floors and followed her through a labyrinth of corridors, but now she halted before a set of heavy double doors, and put a finger to her lips, though she'd been the only one speaking. "Just one moment," she whispered.

Carefully opening the doors, she tiptoed in, then returned a moment later. "You're in luck!" she whispered. "It's the scene where Chief Clark comes to Da'vante for help with his mission!"

She held open the door, finger to lips, and they entered. Will had been in screening rooms before, but this one was closer to the size of an actual theater. It had a dozen rows of plush seats, 80 or 90 in total, though only eight or nine up front were occupied.

After positioning Marjorie's wheelchair in the aisle, with clear sightlines, the dwarf attorney climbed into a seat in the back row.

Sure enough, up there on the screen was Marc Guerin. As the cop, he'd been made up to look somewhat older, and they had him walking with a pronounced limp. But, no doubt about it, the camera loved the bastard!

Where he was walking was down a long, bleak prison corridor, reeking of steely determination as he goes, ignoring the catcalls of the prisoners as he passes their cells. Finally he stops at the cell he's looking for, and an angry voice is heard off camera.

"Fuck you, motherfucker."

"Fuckin' A, Da'vante, thought you might say that." The chief/Marc gives him his familiar, self-effacing grin. "But thought I'd ask for your help anyway."

Da'vante, powerfully built and rage filled, can be seen rising from his cot, and he takes a few steps toward his visitor. "Fuck you motherfucker," he repeats, glaring at him through the bars. "Why should I, who the hell are you?"

The smile again, but now expressing less confidence than confusion. "You're right, Da'vante, that's why I'm here, to try and figure that out." A dramatic beat, and the chief lifts a ribbon over his head, which holds the Congressional Medal of Honor. "The man who killed a dozen so-called terrorists and got this, that's who I *WAS*," he says, displaying the medal to the other. But now, staring into Da'Vante's eyes, he drops the nation's highest award to the floor and slowly grinds it beneath his heel. "But this is who I *AM*."

That was the whole scene. But then it was repeated, with slight variations in tone and inflection; and then it was repeated again, and again after that, as the others in the room presumably decided which one was best.

Tedious at it was, Will knew it would end soon, and unexpectedly he found himself a bit on edge. For all the many notables he had dealt with in his time – governors, mob bosses, hotshot TV reporters – this would be the first international movie star, and this was celebrity of a different magnitude; and he as of yet had no idea what combination of charm, guile and – he hated to think — deference he'd have to use to gain Guerin's confidence.

At last the reel came to an end, and the screen went dark.

"Great fuckin' shit," someone up front pronounced, with authority. "Fuckin' gold!"

"Fantastic work, MG," chimed in one of the others.

Will figured them to be a mix of studio executives, and those directly involved with the film, the director, probably, and some producers; on some movies, there seemed be dozens of those.

"The 'Fuckin' A' line – that was all me!" said a voice unmistakably Guerin's, as the lights came on.

"*You* wrote that dialogue – 'Fuckin' A'?" marveled the first guy, who seemed to be running things.

"Shit, yeah. The script jus' had him walkin' in and askin' for the guy's help. I said no goddamn way, where's my *attitude*?"

"Man, those words – what you wrote – it makes the whole scene," exclaimed a woman in the seat nearby. "Without it the guys' whole relationship makes no sense!"

"Yeah, well that's why I put it in."

"Perfect," agreed another guy. "Because, yeah, at this point these two are still strangers who've been thrown together in the struggle for social justice. But the audience wants to believe they could also be lovers, that it could go that way."

Will looked over at Marjorie, expecting to find a comrade in incredulity, but in her chair in the aisle, she was positively aquiver with excitement.

"Turn on your phone," he whispered.

"How about you, Janice and Jameel," asked the first guy, with an edge of apprehension, "scene work for you?"

"Well, just one thing" replied a younger female, probably no more than 16, with great confidence, "I think Da'vante should be transgender."

"We could do that," the other quickly replied, "that's an easy fix. I mean, so far this is all we've seen of the character."

"Good, do it."

"How about you Jameel, any notes?"

"Just make sure you use a trans actor" – if anything, he sounded younger – "cause cis actors playing LGBTQ characters is never justified ethically or politically."

"Of course, we're well aware, fully understood, will do!"

Will was unable to completely stifle a guffaw. But when the others turned back and saw a dwarf and a woman in a wheelchair, their looks of annoyance were replaced by a half dozen shit-eating grins. All but Janice and Jameel, who shot him daggers.

"Hey," exclaimed Guerin, "you're that little lawyer guy!"

"The name's Tripp," said Will, "Sorry, I listen to the crap you people talk and I can't help laughing."

After a beat, Guerin laughed. "See that's what I hear, he's a real character. I might play him next." He paused. "Puny as he is, they say he's the greatest lawyer ever since Charlie Daniels!"

"That's what they say," agreed Will, and waited to see if anyone would correct him; or, actually, knew better.

"This is my colleague Marjorie Spivak."

"Quite a ride you got there, pretty lady," said Guerin, getting to his feet, and there he was, big as...well, actually, smaller; with his expert eye, the dwarf attorney pegged him at five seven. But already he was striding up the aisle toward Marjorie.

He stopped directly above her, closely studying her chair, as within it, she blushed wildly, far too gone to notice or care.

"Lemme try that!" he said, jerking a thumb over his shoulder. "You, out!"

"I don't think she can walk, MG," ventured one of the studio guys, apologetically.

"I ccccccc-can, too," she said.

"See, that, she ccccccccc-can, too" imitated Marc with a laugh, and then turned back to Marjorie. "Then do it!"

She reached toward him, and with a grunt, launched herself upward, clutching him madly around the neck.

"Whoa, babe, calm down," he laughed, as the others followed, "not *here*." Extricating her hands, he lifted her up and set her down in the aisle. She grabbed an armrest to keep from toppling as he took her place in the chair.

"Oh, yeah, *that's* what I'm talkin' about!" he exclaimed, settling in. "Screw the limp, my guy got fucked up in the war like we say, he's in *this!* For life!"

"Yeah, but see, Marc," said someone, maybe the director, "we have your character beating the shit out of people – and, you know, if he's in a wheelchair..."

"That's ableist bullshit!" shouted Janice angrily.

"Hate speech," agreed Jameel.

"Well, no, I'm sorry, I didn't mean..."

"Someone get this cracker a tape of the damn para-Olympics!"

"Of course, you're right, don't know what I was thinking." He paused, turned back to Guerin. "It's just, see, Marc, I'm afraid the cost would be prohibitive."

"What, this thing can't cost more'n a few grand."

"No, I mean, we'd have to reshoot everything you've done so far."

"Not my problem, asshole, deal with it. All you guys think about is goddamn money — me, I'm talkin' *reality*."

In the momentary silence that followed, Will jumped in. "Gotta say, the man's got a point." They all turned his way. "Look, I'm new at this. And I'm not saying the limp's not great — I totally bought it. But if you're after serious pathos, the kind Marjorie delivers every time she wheels into a courtroom, well..." he nodded at Marc to pick up the cue, and after a confused pause, he did.

"You need the fuckin' chair!"

"You fuckin' *need* it!" echoed Will.

Guerin nodded "See that, this li'l guy's no ass kisser like the rest've you, an' he's an *expert!*" He turned to Will. "You an' me got a whole lot to talk about. Let's get the hell outta here!"

Danny Valenzuela was cruising down Highway 82 south of Abbeville, enjoying the almost otherworldly beauty of the hyacinths and Louisiana irises in the adjacent marshlands, when his phone sounded. He didn't recognize the number.

"I ain't got but one minute, so listen close!"

"Who is...?" he started, but abruptly knew. "I'm listening."

Danny eased the car to a stop on the shoulder.

"You come for the real story, that really it?"

"Right, I'm trying to...?"

"An' first thing you go to that asshole Bayou?"

"Well, you know, from what I heard, *all* you guys were close..."

"Goddamn right, *all* of us! Real close."

"...and you had some pretty interesting times."

"Damn straight! That asshole didn't tell you 'bout that, did he?"

"Not so much..."

"Then you don't know shit." He cackled mirthlessly. "What'll you give me for it?"

"I don't know," said the P.I., caught short, "we could probably discuss that..."

"Cause what I got to say, it could make a whole damn book!"

Danny was familiar with jailhouse braggadocio, but there was something about the way this guy said it...

"It ain't right what they done, we was all suppose to be in this together."

"Right, I understand..." he lied sympathetically. "Well, I'm certainly interested in your side..."

He could almost feel the guy wrestling from inside the prison wall with whatever conscience he had.

"Listen," encouraged Danny, "what I write might lead to a pretty big book deal."

But by then he'd already decided. "Okay, fuck this shit! 'Cause know what, it just ain't right. Be here Thursday, it's visitin' day."

"Got it. Thanks, I look forward to...

The line went dead.

The engine was still running. Putting it back in drive, Danny yanked the car into a u-turn and roared back down the highway toward Lafayette.

Will got into the star's stretch limo first, and quickly scuttled across the plush leather on hands and knees. Guerin followed, settling into his seat and immediately releasing an explosive fart.

"Ahh," said Will, who'd been around animals before, and knew when one was marking his territory, "that even made me feel better."

Guerin smiled. "You li'l fucker, I knew I liked you!"

"Your friends didn't seem crazy about us going out on our own," noted Will, as the car moved into traffic.

"Them guys? They ain't my friends. I know who my friends are, an' it ain't them."

"Where to, Mr. Guerin?" asked the driver over the intercom.

"I tol' you before, asshole!"

"Thank you, sir."

"Business associates, whatever," picked up Will. "Seems like they keep awful close watch over you."

In fact, both one of the studio execs and a guy attached to Third Eye had all but insisted on accompanying them to wherever they were going; one because he had "thoughts on the project," the other because his husband's mother was in town, so he claimed he needed a reason not to go home.

"Almost seems like they don't trust you," noted Will.

"They think I don' know shit from shinola," agreed Guerin. "'Fraid some little shit like you might get their hooks in me 'stead of them."

Will smiled in comradely solidarity. "Well, I always say it's not a bad thing to be underestimated."

"Yeah, me too, I say that," said Guerin tentatively. He paused. "Course, I look bigger on the screen."

Will quickly turned away, pretending to gaze at the passing nightlife on Sunset. "The Sunset Strip," he mused, "heard about it my whole life, and here it is."

"Fuckin' A!"

"Fuckin' A!" agreed Will.

"When I got out here, I couldn't fuckin' believe it."

"I get that."

"Shit, more prime Grade-A pussy on this one block than for 50 miles where I come from!"

Will was at once astonished and delighted by the star's unembarrassed repellence before a total stranger, certain there was a lot more where that came from. "Fuckin' A." He paused. "Well, I'm guessing you get all you can handle."

"Shit, yeah. Only it ain't as easy as before. Like you say, they watch me pretty close."

"Guess it ain't," Will echoed his companion's speech; gauging, correctly, that what someone else might take as mockery, with this guy it would further build trust. "They scared of you, is all…"

"Think so?" said the star in surprise.

"You too damn independent. Me, I'm the same way — spend my whole goddamn life fightin' this shit."

"No shit?"

"The cases I take, the clients, one way or t'other, every one of 'ems takin' on The Man…"

"Fuckin' A!! You *are* a li'l fucker"

"Course, I ain't tellin' you nothin' you don' already know."

The star looked at him blankly.

"Cause that's what our show's all 'bout." He paused, as it hit him. "You seen the treatment, right?"

"Oh, hell, I got people for doin' my readin', I ain't got time for that shit!"

"Fuckin' A!" said Will, understandingly.

"But I seen there was a picture of you in there, I read that. You had a stogie big as a mule's cock in your puny li'l hand, and I said, 'damn, that's one li'l fucker I gotta meet!!'"

"I'm flattered, sir." He reached into his jacket pocket and produced a Cohiba. "Here, have one."

Guerin took it, as with his other hand slapped his knee in delight. "Damn, am I ever takin' you to the right place! Good to know you, li'l man!"

"Good to know you, too, MG."

Will was surprised to note sudden menace in the other's famous blue eyes. "Don't! Only assholes call me that!"

The Grand Havana Room was a relic of a better time, in cities and towns across America done in by the smug do-gooders Will Tripp spent his life fighting, so the dwarf attorney was more than a little surprised to find it in the very heart of Beverly Hills, at Canon and Dayton Way.

The doors of its private elevator opened to a scene of sumptuous ease. Stepping inside, Will took in the rich carpeting, the hand-tooled leather couches and invitingly deep armchairs, the burnished wood bar; and then he sucked in the mixed scent of a dozen of the world's finest cigars wafting over it all.

It was wondrous, a veritable monument to hypocrisy. Far from frowned up, smoking and drinking and scarfing down sirloin was, for its overwhelmingly rich, old, white, male patrons, the payoff for having in their real lives as lawyers, businessmen and studio executives, gulped down all the poisonous crap doled out by the local Jacobins.

The staff was mainly great-looking women.

For Will, it felt like coming home.

Yet within seconds, he was aware of the eyes turning in their direction, and then following them as they were led to a nook in the far side of the room by a stunning blonde.

Guerin, for his part, seemed to take it as his due.

"Come here a lot?" asked Will.

"Yeah, well everythin's comped, so it's a pretty good deal," he replied.

"Many places do that?"

"Shit, yeah, that's all they got in this town, ass kissers."

"Wow, look at that!" Will stopped before an immense, glassed-in humidor, larger any he'd ever seen. It was the glorious beating heart of the place, its *raison d'être*.

"Mind if I take a look?" said Will, and without waiting for a reply, he put his shoulder to the door and pushed it in. Above him, up to the ceiling, loomed polished wood lockers, each bearing a brass nameplate. DeNiro. Nicholson. Schwatznegger.

"Christ, I could live here!" he said, sucking in the intoxicating scent. "You got one?"

"What'd ya think, asshole!" he sneered, insulted. He jerked a thumb and, sure enough, there he was, between Leonardo Di Caprio and Ryan Gosling.

"Funny they put you next to those two," mused the dwarf.

"Pair've assholes," shot back the star, failing to rise to the bait. "Move it, I'm hungry!"

"…Cause I heard from both of 'em this week."

Instantly, he was hyper-focused. "Them fuckers tryin' to steal our show?!"

"Uh uh, no it was about Marjorie."

"Who?"

"The gal in the wheelchair."

He nodded his understanding. "That girl's hot as a pistol, man! Talk about kinky!"

"Fuckin' A," managed Will. "And also a fantastic attorney! Bastards both tryin' to steal her from me, made big offers."

Guerin turned as intense as he ever had on the screen. "Forget that! It's over, she works for me!"

Five minutes later, deep in a leather wingchair, an Arturo Fuente Opus X in hand and a Jack Daniels on the cherry wood table before him, the mercurial star was mellow again.

"Mind if I ask you something, Marc?" ventured his companion.

"Shoot, li'l fucker."

"How do you get away with it?" The other looked confused. "You know, the stuff with women. Even if you ain't doin' nothin', how you talk."

"I'm doin' *plenty*," he returned, anger rising.

"No, no, sure you are, you get all you want."

"Damn right," he said somewhat mollified, though still suspicious. "More! I get more'n *anyone*!"

"It's just that, I mean, this is such a politically correct town, you're not even supposed to *think* those things."

Guerin was already looking bored with the subject, and when a waitress passed, he snapped his fingers, indicating his near empty glass.

"Lookin' good, baby," he said, as she poured, "*juicy*."

"Thank you, Mr. Guerin," she said, blushing.

"How's about we figure out what we gonna do after, you n' me?"

Though her only reply was a shy giggle, as he watched her walk off, Guerin confided: "She's already thinkin' of what excuse to give her boyfriend."

"Wow!" said Will, "impressive!"

"Goddamn right!"

"But, see, it's kind've what I'm talkin' about. I mean, women these days – you gotta know that's a no-go zone…"

That seemed to give him pause. "My manager, he's real smart…"

"Yes, I met him…"

"One time he did tell me not to say pussy, or faggot or ni…"

"Right," Will cut him off, "that's what I mean."

"Least not when one of 'em's around. Said I oughta try'n be *polite.*"

Will nodded. "Only here's the thing. I see what you put out on social media, an' you come across as…"

"Social media? You mean like…" he hesitated.

"Twitter, Instagram, TikTok, the stuff that goes out to your followers…"

"Oh, yeah," he said with pride, "I got somethin' like ten million."

"Actually, it's more like 25."

"Well, fuck me!" he exclaimed, pleased, "you know more'n I do!"

The fact had been working its way toward Will's consciousness for some time, but only now did it hit him with absolute clarity. "You don't write that…"

"Shit, no, why would I?"

"Who does?"

"Christ, you think I know the name of every li'l fucker on the payroll…"

"Those two at the dailies. Janice an'…"

"Them, I guess, but there's a whole team of 'em." He paused, and repeated what obviously he'd been told. "You gotta do that, that's what the fans want."

"Sure."

"I don' bother with that shit, I'm all about the fuckin' *art*."

"So you didn't put out anything about Mike Sawyer…"

"Who?"

"The actor?" He waited for some sign of recognition. "You know: 'It ain't luck, it's Providential?'"

"Him? Love that fucker!"

"He was gonna be your co-star in *New Orleans*."

There was again a blank look, but this time it passed quickly. "Right, that piece of shit. Yeah, I was thinkin' maybe I'd play the fag pirate an' blow Johnny Depp outta the fuckin' water."

"Jean Lafitte? He wasn't gay!"

"You shittin' me, with *that* name? But, anyways…" He waved his hand to indicate he'd lost interest in the project, moved on to other things.

"That team of yours really went after Sawyer hard, you know that? Fucked him over bad, under your name."

"Oh, yeah?" He sipped his whiskey. "Them's the breaks, guess they gotta do what they gotta do."

The dwarf lawyer nodded, and fell silent, but what he was thinking was: *Me, too.*

Known as Angola, the Louisiana State Penitentiary was the nation's largest maximum security facility, and Danny Valenzuela had long been aware of its reputation. As one civil liberties journal had it, Angola "has historically been the most brutalizing institution of its kind in the nation."

Still, seeing it up close drove home the point in a way mere words never could. From the parking lot, the massive prison loomed over the landscape like a grim medieval castle, barbed wire ringing the top, officers with submachine guns manning the corner turrets.

Where it was a given that at every such institution the strong ruled the weak with crude impunity, behind these walls, murder and suicide remained so commonplace that those in charge sometimes scarcely bothered to make the distinction.

As the P.I. walked toward the visitors' entrance, Styrofoam coffee cup in hand, he could see stretching out beyond the 18 thousand acres given over to factories and working farms. Here, it was said, prisoners were worked so hard that some became so desperate to escape they'd sever their own Achilles heels with rusty razors.

Apparently, Yoda was one of those ready to do anything to get out.

More than an hour before the 9 a.m. opening, there was already a line along the wall by the visitors' entrance, over-whelmingly women, and mostly black. Danny got behind a young woman, no more than 18, who turned to him, perplexed.

"I think lawyers can jus' go right in," she offered.

"That's okay, I'm a visitor. I'll wait my turn."

Once inside, he took his place on a bench, waiting for his name to be called for processing. When others who'd entered after him began getting called in before he was, he was at first perplexed, then annoyed. He'd actually been pretty sure the woman on line had it right, that his appearance would afford him favored treatment; but it was apparently the opposite.

"Mr. Richard Hernandez?"

Jolted to awareness, he walked to the battered desk at the front of the room, phony ID in hand. Knowing the guy he was to see was a hard case, he hoped they'd forego a full cavity search. He'd have no contact with the prisoner, anyway; they'd face each other through a solid inch of plastic.

"Mr. Hernandez?" said the officer behind the desk.

"Yes,"

"One moment please." He rose and disappeared through the door behind, returning a moment later with a harried looking man of about 50 in a light brown suit.

"Mr. Hernandez," he said, "I understand you're here to see Mr. Leroy."

"That's right."

"My name is Harris, I'm a staff psychologist here at LSP. Would you be a relative?"

"No, I'm not."

"A friend?"

"Actually, I'm a reporter. He's agreed to talk to me about a story I'm working on."

At this, the other seemed to visibly flinch. "I see. Would you come with me, please?"

He led him back through the door, into what turned out to be the offices of the prison administration. The harsh fluorescent lighting and warren of small, cramped offices called to mind an insurance concern in old fashioned black and white movies.

They stopped before an open door and Harris knocked. The woman within, in her early 30s and surprisingly attractive, looked up at them and smiled.

"Barbara, this is Mr. Hernandez – Claude Leroy's visitor." He paused and added meaningfully, "He's a journalist."

She stood, still smiling. "I see. A journalist. For whom?"

"*The New York Post*. What's going on here? He's expecting me."

"Barbara is our public affairs officer," said Harris, the psychologist, who retreated from the room, closing the door behind him.

"May I ask what you're writing about?"

"It has to do with crime."

She nodded, unsurprised, they were in a prison. "And prison life?"

"I don't think so. Not much. I think that's between him and me."

She hesitated, then shot him an odd, reflexive smile. "I'm afraid there was an...*incident* this morning."

"An incident?" But the way she had said it left little doubt. "Something happened to him?"

"In the shower...with shivs. It was pretty bad." She paused. "He didn't...*make* it."

Seeing him blanch, she instantly went into P.R. overdrive. "I don't know how much research you've done, but you will find incidents like this are all too common. Everywhere. In fact, with the reforms that have been made here, in recent years our record on violent assaults among prisoners has been far, *far* better than is generally understood – we're actually ranked in the top half nationally."

He nodded blankly.

"So I very much hope you won't blow this out of proportion. It's very easy to make a prison a whipping boy – easy, but wrong."

"Do they know who did it?"

"Not yet. They know where all the surveillance cameras are; the courts have ruled they're entitled to their private spaces."

He shook his head. "Right."

"There will be an investigation, we will certainly find out." She paused. "May I ask how well you knew Mr. Leroy?"

"Not very."

"Frankly, I understand he was a rotten apple. He made himself quite a few enemies. That's not an excuse, of course, but it's the truth, so bear it in mind."

It was a tossup whose information was more startling. But without much reflection, the dwarf lawyer decided it had to be his. Cons got shanked every day; he'd had clients it happened to, usually guys who deserved it.

"Sure," acknowledged the P.I. in response to this observation, "but not like this. I'm not a big believer in coincidence."

Nodding, Will conceded the point; neither was he. "You're probably right," he allowed, "It was you that got him killed, your visit."

"It was a hit, pure and simple."

"Certainly seems that way."

"Yoda was off the reservation."

"Uh huh."

"The question is what he had that was so dangerous…?"

"And who was so eager to keep it under wraps."

The P.I. looked at him closely. Not only was the answer obvious, it was precisely the one they were hoping for and seeking: Marc Guerin. Indeed, in the P.I.'s mind, the case was coming together beautifully. With everything he'd built at stake, and tens of millions in future earnings, the star had seen to it his old friend was silenced. Sure, he'd acted through surrogates closer to the scene, most likely Broussard. But

Bayou was nothing more than a half-assed fur trapper, for chrissakes, and such a hit wouldn't have come cheap.

Then, again, Valenzuela hadn't met Guerin, and his boss had.

"I'm guessing he doesn't know a thing," said Will.

"Impossible."

"You gotta understand...I know it's hard to believe... but beyond the arrogance and insecurity and mean spiritedness, there is *nothing* there."

"You're saying..."

"*Nothing. Nada.* It's not just that he's a moron, that goes without saying, but no *soul*. The Marc Guerin the world knows is a total fabrication — every so-called 'thought,' every supposedly human impulse, every action..."

"You think it's Broussard..."

"No question he's involved – like you say, he's on the scene. But I'm guessing it's also the people out here, protecting their investment..."

The P.I. slowly nodded. While he had some catching up to do on the individuals involved, he recognized what the other was saying was entirely plausible; for, like the dwarf attorney, he knew how ready were those wielding power on the other side of the ideological divide to do anything, to anyone, and justify it as serving the greater good.

"So you've got Arthur working for Guerin's manager...?" said Danny, putting two and two together.

Will nodded. "Actually, technically, the manager's working for him."

"So he has access to inside information?"

"That's the thing — not yet. Can you believe it, they won't give him the passwords — the president of the fucking company! Disgraceful! Flat out racism!"

"So what does he do all day?"

"What do any of them do? He has meetings – with producers, agents, packagers, who the hell knows who? He shows his *face* – which is really all the guy wants! Sits on his ass racking up big expense accounts. But Arthur's let him know he's not happy, this isn't what he signed up for, he's making noises about suing."

"Arthur is?"

"Proud of the guy, he's really showing initiative. He actually had it written into his contract that if he's fired he gets two million, and will get a mill if he leaves by his own volition."

"Arthur did that?" said the P.I., impressed.

"I tell you, he's really grown! And Marjorie, too – we got her working directly for Guerin as a backup, and she has the same contract." He paused. "Now, the next step on your end...."

"I know," the P.I. cut him off. "It's the part of the job I hate most, but I'm on it."

Heading south on Rte. 167 toward Varennes, Valenzuela war-gamed the coming encounter. But, really, this time the exercise was pointless. It didn't seem there was any approach that had much of a shot. Offering condolences? Saying it was as much of a shock to him as to them? That he had no idea this might happen?

Jesus, he had *made* it happen, they knew that as well as he did. Nor, all things considered, was it entirely a surprise.

He parked where he had earlier, and this time didn't ring the bell, but walked directly to the yard behind the trailer. Momentarily, he was relieved to see the father in his chair, like before. Only this time he wasn't reading, just staring vacantly into space, with what the P.I. took to be a look of inexpressible sadness.

Then he spotted Danny.

"You!"

"Mr. Leroy, I'm so sorry for your loss." Even to his own ears, the words rang unbelievably trite.

"What're you after now?"

"I just, you know, I wanted to know if you have any idea about why, you know, this…happened."

The older man stared at him.

"At least that's something we can do for him, try to get him justice."

He stood there uncomfortably as the dead man's father just stared.

"I don' know who you are, mister, or what you want," he finally spoke, deliberately. "You didn't know my boy from a hole in the wall…"

"No, that's true, sir, I didn't…"

"Well, lemme tell ya, it ain't worth your trouble. Claude was bad news, wasn't no one's fault but his own. You know what all this means to me, that he's gone…?"

He shook his head. "No, sir."

"It's a *relief*, is what it is. Now we don' have to worry 'bout him no more."

"Ronald, stop!"

Danny turned to Leroy's mother, and saw that this time she wasn't angry, just defeated.

"We loved our boy!" she said firmly. "If you write about him, write that!"

"I will. Yes, ma'am."

"He knew what he was doin', he tol' us he wanted to see you. I tol' him not to, in no uncertain terms, but he's not someone you can reason with."

He noted the present tense; she still hadn't fully absorbed it. "Any idea what he wanted to tell me…?"

"Jus' his side've it, is all, that Marc Guerin was as much his friend as Kevin Broussard's." She hesitated. "I know it waxed his ass for sure that Kevin got Beau Rivage, he never got past that one."

"Beau Rivage?"

"Plantation down by St. Elizabethville," said her husband.

"Claude, went on an' on 'bout that, he knew for damn sure it weren't no nutria pelts that paid for it. An' all Claude wanted was a halfway decent lawyer."

"No lawyer was gonna help him," said her husband gently. "It was the damn drugs, he did it to his own self."

Danny stood there a moment, wondering how to ask, but didn't have to.

"He left some stuff with us," she said. "Take a look, if you want. No good to us now, all jus' goin' to the Goodwill."

"Thank you, I appreciate that."

There wasn't much, all of it took up no more than half a closet in the trailer's back bedroom, and the P.I., a regular patron of his local Goodwill in the Bronx, guessed that even a rural outpost wouldn't be much interested. It was mainly old pants and sweatshirts, several worn pairs of shoes, as well as some random paperbacks, including, oddly, several Star Trek novelizations. Too, there was a soccer trophy marked "Participant" that made Valenzuela smile – lot of good *that* did for his self-esteem!

But then, in the corner, half hidden beneath another sweatshirt, he spotted a shoebox. It was labeled, in Magic Marker, "MG." Opening the lid, he was disappointed to see clippings about the actor from the usual places. But then came the surprise: the article from the student paper in Pennsylvania! And written in ink in the margin, in Marc Guerin's childish hand: "Look who's a fucking star!"

And beneath that the articles, unlabeled but bound together by a rubber band, were three old VHS tapes.

A week later, Danny arrived in L.A.

Will's trusted friend and financial advisor, Marty Katz, was already on the scene, having shown up a day earlier, along with Will's brother Bennett, who'd hitched a ride on Katz's chartered Gulfstream G700. With Arthur XXX and Marjorie already close at hand, each with a great job and no evident responsibilities, free to come and go at will, the dwarf lawyer had his full war council in place.

For security's sake, they met outside of town, at a Motel 6 in suburban Ontario, where even the most reckless Hollywood player was unlikely to ever risk being seen.

By now they all had the information on Beau Rivage, and had seen the photos of the antebellum plantation, with its imposing multi-columned front and oak-shaded alleys. Although technically owned by Good Buddy Enterprises, an LLC with a Delaware address, it was indeed home to Kevin Broussard, his four children, his wife and his mistress. Moreover, it had been learned that Broussard was on the Zydeco Productions' payroll, listed as "advisor/locations scout," receiving a monthly fee of $42,550, plus unspecified expenses, and use of two company vehicles.

This information had been procured not by Third Eye Synergistics president Arthur XXX, who was still locked out of the company's files, but by Marjorie. "Working" at Zydeco Productions' office on the Precision lot, she'd wandered into the storeroom and happened upon 12 years of company financial statements, sent monthly by the accounting firm DiMichel-Mittelman Associates, which Guerin tossed into a blue plastic tub without bothering to open.

In the motel's deserted breakfast room, arrayed around several Formica tables pulled together, the team considered how to proceed.

"So," said Katz, "the obvious question is: What does Broussard have on this guy that his silence is worth" – the landlord did the math in his head – "$510,600 per annum, plus expenses?"

"Not bad," whistled Arthur, of the quick calculation.

"Half a mil?" said Katz, misunderstanding. "Walking around money for Guerin. Almost makes me wonder if the information is all that hot."

"Hey," countered Valenzuela, who'd come to feel protective of his recent stomping grounds, "we're not talking New York or L.A. prices, half a million in Lafayette you can get a six bedroom house, *three bathrooms,* for what I pay for a one bedroom apartment in Riverdale!"

"It's the market," snapped Katz defensively. "It's called capitalism."

"I'm not arguing, I agree with you."

"Or maybe it's not a payoff at all…"

They all turned to Bennett.

"Maybe it's just that since he'd succeeded, Guerin wanted to share his success with his best friend. He wants to pay it forward."

The landlord slapped his forehead in stupification, but Will nodded approvingly at his brother; he knew how important it was never to forget how much the world was in the hands of those who actually thought this way.

Encouraged, Bennett added: "I'm just saying let's not assume the worst. Rule one of conflict resolution is most people are basically good."

"Okay, Bennett, enough!" snapped the dwarf lawyer. He gazed around the table at the others. "Actually, I wouldn't be sure Guerin even knows about it. It could be the studio. Or his management." He paused. "Anyway, Bennett comes close to having a point. Wherever the money's coming from, those payments are not illegal. We can be damn sure the lawyers and accountants have seen to that."

"What matters is *why*?" Valenzuela returned to the issue at hand. "What don't they want the world to know? What could be so bad they'd kill to keep it hidden?" He opened his computer screen. "And we think we know."

"Of the three videotapes Danny got out of the murdered guy's place," picked up Will, "one had nothing useful, it's just a Lafayette TV station's coverage of a Mardi Gras parade."

"2013," pointed out the P.I., "Guerin was king, and the other three guys were up on the float with him, so you can see why he kept it. Might've been the last time they were all together."

"But the other two…" said Will, as he hit the key to bring up a video on the screen computer, and there appeared a frozen image of a serious looking anchorwoman with bouffant hair, sitting before the KLFY News logo. "The first one you'll see is from…"

"…June 20, 1999," said Valenzuela, reading from his notepad. He looked up. "Guerin would have been 13."

Will hit another key, catching the anchorwoman in midsentence.

"…of curious and disturbing news from St. Elizabethville in Iberville Parish. Carlos McGee has a report."

The reporter stood on a deserted rural road in a trench coat, microphone in hand. "It has been three days now since 19-year-old Dwayne Baker and his 18-year-old girlfriend, Catherine Sloan, set off from Catherine's house in Varennes to go to a movie at the St. Elizabethville Mall. They apparently never made it. After the worried parents contacted police, their car, a green 2003 Oldsmobile Aurora, was found abandoned here, on light travelled Route 201. Police have impounded the car, and it is being inspected for possible evidence. But as of now, the teens' disappearance remains a mystery. Lafayette police urge anyone with information to contact them at the tips hotline – 1-800-SAFETY1. Carlos McGee, KLFY News."

Immediately, there appeared a second report, from reporter Wanda Smith of Lafayette's other local station, KATC, providing essentially the same information.

Next, came the following day's story from Carlos McGee, reporting on the progress of the investigation; the teens were still missing and the impounded vehicle had provided no leads. This, too, this was followed by Wanda Smith with a similar report.

By now the meaning of what they were seeing was apparent to all present, with the possible exception of Bennett.

"How many of these are there?" asked Arthur XXX simply, shaking his head.

"Fourteen in all. It was a big story for a while, 'til they lost interest."

Indeed, the next report was from station WWL out of New Orleans, featuring the missing girl's distraught mother, and over the next several times over the weeks they, too, provided updates on the story. With hopes fading that the teens would be found unharmed, police sources speculated that it had been a robbery gone awry, or perhaps a botched kidnapping. But there was no hard evidence for either, and the final report on the tape was August 4, six weeks after the teens went missing.

Those around the table waited in silence as the scene went dark.

"What's next is from the other tape..." said the dwarf attorney, as another reporter, a young black man, appeared on screen, standing beside a body of brackish water. In his sports jacket and tie he was obviously more up-to-date, and the image itself was crisper, the color less garish.

"Thanks, Jennifer," he was saying. "This was indeed quite an unsettling find here on Avery Island. An apparently human bone, discovered right here, on the bank of a salt marsh heavily populated by alligators. As you know, Avery Island is a popular tourist destination here in Iberville Parrish, as well as home to the famous Tabasco sauce, and it is no exaggeration to say the locals here are quite unsettled by the find. We are told the bone, which is in poor condition, appears to be the femur, or leg bone, of a female, approximately 15 to 30 years of age. Police are going through their files of missing persons to see if they can find a match. This is Jackson Starke, KFLY News."

Will turned off the computer. "That's it. There was nothing else on that tape."

"It was a match with Catherine Sloan," added Valenzuela, before anyone asked. "But it didn't lead to any arrests."

"Christ, almighty!" exclaimed Katz. "They did it! They killed those kids."

Will nodded. "And kept the tapes as a trophy. How long was this before they hit that truck, and beat the crap out've the driver for no damn reason?"

"Almost exactly two months to the day. They were *seriously* bad dudes." He paused, shook his head. "But try telling them that down there."

He had tried, of course, but with nothing to go on beyond old taped news reports and his intuition, it had been worse than useless. Hearing the name Marc Guerin, the D.A. in Plaquemine, seat of Iberville Parrish, had refused to hear a word more.

"*Chicos*, I can't tell you how it is down there — this guy Guerin is untouchable, a god. I was lucky to get out've that goddamn office without getting' slapped in cuffs myself."

There was a long moment of silence.

"That's okay," pronounced Will finally, "it ain't the good folks of *Louisiana* we fixin' to get riled up anyways, is it?"

Andrew Craig was stunned to hear Will Tripp on the other end of the line, but if there's anything the veteran journalist was good at, it was keeping his cool.

"Mr. Tripp, I heard you were in town…"

"Not surprised. I assume you know everything that happens in this part of the world…"

"Well, that's my job."

"…If not in the *entire* world."

Craig chuckled, he took it as his due, though he certainly never expected it from this quarter.

Like so many high-profile members of his debased profession, Craig was a product of the activist '60s, which is to say, frankly proclaimed himself a powerful force for good. By virtue of hard work and a gift for office politics, he'd long ago landed a thrice-weekly column on the Op-ed page of the powerful *Los Angeles Times*, which had given him both renown and a devoted following of like-minded nitwits.

But that was almost 30 ago now, and while for many Craig's name still registered as familiar, he had long since been eclipsed by a variety of bloggers, Tweeters, influencers and others who'd come to prominence in social media. His column was down to once a week, and, indeed, his publication itself had a circulation barely a third of what it had once been, and that composed overwhelmingly of readers over 60.

In short, Craig was yesterday's news – over.

And Will Tripp, who'd dealt with his sad sort many, many times, knew how much it was killing him.

"So what can I do for you?" asked the journalist, as ever playing the big man.

"I have something for you. Potentially something big."

"Oh, yeah," he said, with faux nonchalance. "What might that be?"

"Not over the phone."

"How soon can you get out to Malibu?"

Will smiled – Jeez, the bastard really had grown fat and lazy; that's what came from getting force fed material by press agents and bedmates on the left.

"Forget it, I'll give it to someone else."

"No, no, wait, I'm free. What works for you?"

Will could already picture him getting off his fat ass and making for his car.

"Santa Monica beach, by the pier, in 45 minutes."

Will got to the appointed spot a few minutes early, and gazed about with satisfaction. The natural wonder that it had been was an eyesore; calamitous living proof of the insanity of liberal social policy, it was a vast homeless camp; a dumping ground for the mentally ill, addicted and otherwise desperate, wandering about aimlessly or huddled in makeshift shanties.

A few minutes later, watching the unkempt, heavyset journalist huff his way toward him on the sand, he was reminded of Chris Farley as the motivational speaker guy on SNL.

"Beautiful place," he greeted Craig, his outstretched little arm taking in the surroundings.

"Sure is!" said Craig, oblivious, as he tried to catch his breath. "What d'you got?"

Will wagged a finger, for the other to stoop low, and when he did, with effort, the dwarf adopted a conspiratorial tone. "I'm not sure about this. Can I trust you…?"

The reporter nodded, he could understand that. "All I can give you is my word."

"Look, I know you're a fair-minded guy, that's why I called. There are other people I could've gone to, people on my side, but I went to you because you have so much greater reach, and a lot more power."

The other *loved* that. "And I pride myself on using it wisely."

"I know that, I've always respected your integrity," allowed Will.

"Just for the record, I've always felt the same about you."

During all this, Craig had been eyeing the manila envelope in Will's tiny hand.

"Look," he said, "all I can give you is my word, I hope it's good enough." He paused, extending an eager hand. "Please…"

Will held on to the envelope, but took a deep breath, indicating he'd decided. "It's about Marc Guerin…"

"Oh?" said Craig, with interest. "What about him?"

The dwarf lawyer opened the envelope slowly, and withdrew the article from the student paper. "This," he said, and handed it over.

Craig's eyes hungrily scanned the page. The parts about his career in porn had been highlighted in yellow.

"This is genuine, you're sure of that?" he said, without looking up. "You've verified this?"

"One hundred percent. Talk to Marc, he'll probably give you even more detail. He's proud of it, it's not like he's the first guy in the business who got started this way."

"And plenty have done a lot worse," he said, with an unexpected flash of humor. "Great stuff! Thanks!"

No doubt he would claim credit for unearthing this juicy bit of cinematic history.

"There's other stuff in there that might also be of interest," added Will nonchalantly, "it has to do with the crowd he hung with back in Louisiana…"

"Oh, yeah? How so?"

"Take a look," said the dwarf attorney, turning to walk off, "if you decide to go there, I might be able to point you in the right direction."

No way at this point he was about to reveal what else his P.I. had unearthed. Better to see if the old reporter still had the *cajones*, or was desperate enough, to do some actual digging on his own.

Recognizing he'd been challenged, Craig was staring back down at the page, and Will quickened his pace. It would take him maybe three minutes to get to the part about the truck robbery, and he wanted to be gone by then.

Will was halfway back to the Valley in his limo when his phone sounded.

"You miserable little bastard!"

"Hey, there, Noah," he greeted his agent.

"You're fucking *done* in this town! *Finished*! I just heard from the studio!!!"

The dwarf attorney sensed what this was about, and though he was disappointed, he was also already enjoying the tantrum. "You're saying they don't want *Attorney for the Damned*?" he asked, with deep disappointment.

"Don't play dumb, you fucker! There are standards, you don't get away with pulling this shit!"

"Wait, I'm confused, what shit is this…?"

"Don't deny it! You're trying to use the media to smear Marc fucking Guerin!"

"Oh, *that*…"

"Thank God the guy you went to has some fucking integrity! Jesus F. Christ, after I put you in touch with these people!!!"

"Yeah, that was a mistake on your part."

"It's almost like you were using the show as a ruse!"

"Hey, you always knew Michael was my client."

He paused. "Hold on, wait. I'm *right,* it *was* a fucking ruse?"

"Yep, a ruse," said Will, starting to like the sound of the word himself.

"I LOVE it! You're a fucking *genius*! Next time we pitch the show, we'll use it!"

"Wait, didn't you just say…"

"There are other studios, for fuck's sake, there're guys who'll buy it just to see Precision take one up the ass!"

"Look, Noah, there's not gonna be any show."

"No show? Now you're being completely unreasonable."

"Jesus, don't you have the balls to even hold a grudge!"

The agent burst out laughing. "God, I just love it when you…"

There came the beep of another call – Sue Sawyer – and Will took it.

"Sue, I was about to call, I need to give you a heads up."

"I know what's going on, and I don't want ANY part of this."

"What have you heard?" he asked with concern, astonished at how quickly word got around.

"I think you know," she said. "And I do not want to be connected with this in ANY way. Do I make myself clear?"

He'd thought at first she was distraught, but no, this was more like anger.

"Right, you no longer want to be involved with the case."

"It's Michael's problem, not mine. I'm moving forward, I'm trying to reestablish my career."

"I see."

"I've left him, I'm getting a divorce."

"Really?"

"On the strong recommendation of my agent. And my therapist. And our daughter's advisor at Chester College – she's been deeply traumatized by her father's behavior!"

"Fine, if that's your decision," he said. "Where's Michael now?

"I can't tell you, no longer my problem." She paused. "You might try Santa Monica beach."

As always, Will had a Plan B.

Sad End for Star's Boyhood Pals, ran the headline on Page Six, *The New York Post*'s widely read daily feature.

"In a twist that might have come from a Hollywood thriller," it began, "sources reveal that two of superstar Marc Guerin's closest friends during his misspent boyhood in rural Louisiana met deaths that left more questions than answers."

Planting the item had not been a problem. The dwarf lawyer had long enjoyed a fruitful relationship with the feisty tabloid – sympathetic if sometimes over-the-type hyperbolic coverage of his cases in exchange for special access. Moreover, in this case, Danny Valenzuela had conducted much of his research that led to the story under its auspices.

"The members of the group gave one another nicknames," read the item's key paragraph, "with Leroy known as 'Yoda,' Peedee as 'Tiny' and Guerin as 'Li'l Man,' since he was younger than the rest. Nevertheless, by the star's own account, published in a student newspaper in 1998, he participated with the two, in addition to a third older boy, in what he termed 'hijinx.' Among these was the robbery of a delivery truck, for which the others did jail time. Yet, apparently due to his youth, Guerin got off with only a wrist tap."

Everything in the story was fully verifiable. It, of course, made no mention of the missing teens.

Still, there was plenty there, and the dwarf lawyer and his team eagerly awaited the reaction.

But over the next few days, there was nothing – the story was ignored by other media, from major mainstream publications to gossip sites on social media. By collective agreement, it was effectively buried.

In fact, as far as Will could ascertain, it received only one notable mention – in Andrew Craig's column that Sunday.

In the fairy tale world of Hollywood foisted on an unsuspecting public back in the Forties and Fifties, Rock Hudson was the most eligible bachelor in town and Judy Garland everyone's girl next door. Today we know better – and we're all better off for it. We know that stars lead real and very complex lives. We know they can be gay and happy; or come home after a hard day on the set and medicate themselves into a stupor. In short, we know that they do not always lead the lives that the narrowest minds would like them to lead.

The press is largely responsible for this new understanding, and those who have reported honestly and fairly on the business of entertainment in recent years deserve our thanks.

But in journalism, as elsewhere in this coarsened moment, the hard work of getting it right too often falls prey to the hunger for the quick and easy score. Which brings us to Marc Guerin, increasingly regarded as among our finest screen actors, and the second rate tabloid, long given to peddling the tired right-wing myth of 'liberal' Hollywood, currently yapping at his heels. In a land where fairness and simple decency were the norm, it is this, not anything in the estimable Mr. Guerin's hardscrabble past, that would be criminal!

It went on in this vein, driven equally by pique and that its author could dash it out without leaving his bedroom. He conluded:

We've gotten so used to thinking of stars as royalty, we start to believe they're not entitled to the same protections as everyone else. But it's time we wised up. For when a Marc Guerin is mercilessly smeared, for sport or for profit, the very spirit of the First Amendment is corrupted. And when we allow that to happen, it is not just a brilliant young star who is the victim, but all of us.

Will fleetingly hoped that, however inadvertently, Craig might have served his purposes. But, no, no one paid attention to his column, either; probably because, ignorant of the original story, they had not the slightest idea what the suck-up was going on about.

For Will's crew, this was rock bottom, never had he seen any of them so deeply dispirited.

Well, no, that wasn't strictly true. Depression, laced with generalized anger at the world, was pretty much the normal state of affairs for his friend Marty Katz, the New York City landlord. In fact, Marty seemed, in his fashion, almost heartened by developments, grimly satisfied that others were at last starting to see things his way.

"I look at this town, and you know what I see?" he said bitterly. "The Bronx Housing Court writ large!"

"To you the whole world is the Bronx Housing Court..." said Valenzuela.

"Yes, more and more every day! But this place," he declared with finality, "is the worst of the worst! If you're not one of them, *a good person*, you're dead. No appeal! The Bronx Housing Court!"

"Meanwhile Guerin's untouchable," said the P.I.

"Yes! An armed robber, probably a murderer, and no one cares! Because he's a *good* person!"

Valenzuela knew he was being egged on, but he didn't care. "You're right, that *hijo de puta* could shoot a man in broad daylight..."

"…A child, strangle him! A little baby!"

"…And they'd applaud!"

"Give him one of their goddamn awards! Best support-ing child killer!"

The others listened without comment. They'd been here in Will's hotel suite for hours already, brought together to plot their next move, and they'd come up with nothing. There were plastic cups and paper plates with pizza residue on every surface. Arthur and even Bennett had moved from beer to whiskey. Hoping it might spark some inspiration, Will had set KLFY's coverage of the Mardi Gras parade to running on a loop on the TV, but by now only Marjorie was paying any attention to Guerin and his three friends in their cheesy royal get-up.

Indeed, if anything, the sight of that tumultuous scene had served only to depress them even further, serving as a reminder of how quickly, and catastrophically, things had changed for the worse. Apparently, back in 2013, women had not only liked men, but readily embraced even obvious creeps with lusty abandon; and trannies were not just content, but fabulous, confined to their own weirdo lane; and before Black Lives Matter or systemic racism, blacks and whites got along fine, even in the wake of a tough national election.

"Damn it, you two!" Will cut off the gripe session between the landlord and P.I., "that's not why we're here!"

He himself had every confidence that by day's end they'd come up with something. There were always options, and he always found them. If nothing else, he had the tapes secretly made in the offices of the agent and studio honcho, nakedly revealing their contempt for diversity of thought. Those could be edited into a compelling and devastating documentary more powerful than anything that fat bastard Michael Moore had ever done.

Then, again, he also realized, things being as they are, such a documentary would never get the kind of mass distribution the fat bastard's had; or, in all likelihood, make it beyond the conservative ghetto.

In fact, at that moment the dwarf lawyer was feeling something he'd rarely felt in all his years fighting the good fight. It was uncomfortably close to hopelessness, and he knew it had to be resisted. He knew people by the millions felt it every time they turned on the news, or learned what their children had been taught that day in school, or were subjected to yet another lecture from a Hollywood moron, but that giving in to it could lead to no good.

Sitting on the bed, surveying the scene, the dwarf lawyer had just reached for the near empty bottle of Jack Daniels on the bedside table, when he was startled by Marjorie's scream.

"LLLLLOOOOOK!!!"

She was pointing at the TV screen.

"What?" said Will, hurrying down from the bed. "Quick, run it back." Valenzuela did. There were Guerin and his friends in costume, laughing, obviously having a blast, when in the background, ever more prominent as the float approached, could be seen a black man and white woman, together with their small son, all of them prominently wearing buttons with the smiling face of the new president. Spotting them, Guerin's expression changes, then, laughing, he shoots them the finger, and turns back to his friends.

Will had moved within inches of the screen. "What'd he say? Run it again in slow motion!!!"

A moment later, there could be no doubt, so clear were the words on the star's lips.

A deep peace settled over the dwarf lawyer as Marjorie spoke them.

"FFFFFFUUUUCK OBAMA!"

As a First Amendment absolutist, Will stressed that he had no interest in infringing upon anyone's expression of opinion; in fact, in this case was willing to assist in spreading that opinion far and wide.

It took Precision Pictures and Zydeco Productions less than a day to green light *New Orleans,* and reinstate Michael Sawyer as co-star. In the press release announcing this decision, the film's other star and Zydeco's president, Marc Guerin, called Sawyer "an actor of astonishing range and an individual of deep and abiding integrity. All too frequently in these complicated times, some are quick to condemn others. But we must never forget that each of us has the right to be judged as an individual, based solely on his, her, or eirs character."

The star was widely praised for his courage, *Time* featuring him on the cover the following week, under the heading: A Screen Hero Speaks Truth to Power.

The party thrown for Sawyer by Zydeco and Third Eye Synergistics at Guerin's Ojai ranch was the town's hottest invite in months, attended by scores of industry players.

The dwarf lawyer was unable to make it – also he had not been invited – but he was live streaming the event aboard his

Gulf Stream on the tarmac at what would surely not much longer be John Wayne Airport, waiting to take off, when Noah Field rose to make a toast.

"We are indeed a village," proclaimed the agent, one arm flung over Sawyer's shoulder, the other over Sue's, "a village full of good and loving souls, who get up every morning and go to work with just one thing in mind: making the world a better place." He paused meaningfully. "Welcome back, Mike Sawyer – and fuck you all!"

Will sat back as the plane started down the runway, a Cohiba in hand, his whiskey sour jiggling on the table before him, and reflected. Taking on the cutthroat crybabies at *The New York Times*, and their insane 1619 Project, already felt like a relief.

Harry Stein is the author of twelve books, both fiction and nonfiction. His best-selling *How I Accidentally Joined the Vast Right-Wing Conspiracy (and Found Inner Peace)*, charting his own transition from Left to Right, was particularly influential, establishing him as a writer who takes on serious subjects with wit and humor; combining, as even acknowledged *The New York Times* (at the time still marginally reputable), "a smart aleck's nerve and a prophet's boldness." It was followed by *I Can't Believe I'm Sitting Next to a Republican; No Matter What They'll Call This Book Racist*; and the first in the Will Tripp series, *Will Tripp, Pissed Off Attorney-at-Law*.

CPSIA information can be obtained
at www.ICGtesting.com
Printed in the USA
LVHW030732250621
691046LV00006B/203/J

9 781735 192802